UNDER FIRE

SHAWNA COLEING

Chapter 1

CLARA'S STRIDE didn't slow as she dipped to grab the basket by the door. Once outside, she paused on the top step to breathe deeply of the autumn smells that hung in the air. It was one of the first cool days of the season and hinted at the cold air on the horizon.

Winter couldn't come soon enough. As usual, the hot summer had brought heavy humidity and a rash. She scratched at the remains of the red inflammation on the inside of her elbow.

Not only did the coming months mean colder temperatures that better suited her heavy frame, but it also meant her husband would be away from the house more. And less of Simon was better for all of them, including Franky, who had been spending more time with his dad in the shed.

She slid the basket up her arm and headed for the chickens. They were laying well lately.

Before she was halfway across the yard, a loud bang reverberated from the shed nearby. She stopped and held her breath instead of gluing her eyes to the ground and continuing with her chores like she knew she should have. But nowhere was safe when Simon was in one of his rages and she didn't want the chickens to bear any of the fallout.

The door to the shed flew open, and her husband stood there, nostrils flaring. Then he caught sight of Clara.

"What are you lookin' at?" he said, his eyes narrowing.

This time she did drop her eyes to the ground. "Nothin'. Just gettin' some eggs."

"Blasted eggs again? Are you that dim in the head you can't come up with anything else to make? I knew I shoulda married Sylvia Barton. Now, that woman knew how to cook."

"I can make you somethin' else if you don't want—"

He plowed toward her, and she recoiled when he grabbed the basket she was carrying. She tried to slip her arm out of the way, but he twisted as he yanked. Pain exploded in her shoulder, stealing her breath. She grunted but bit her tongue so she didn't cry out. Her face contorted in agony as she sucked air in through her nose to regain control.

He spat at her. "Don't you start yer whining, you worthless sack of dirt. Do you know what I endure every day putting up with you? I don't know why I waste my time. I coulda done anything with my life, but I'm stuck here with you."

Fear and fury wound themselves around Clara, tightening a place in her chest that she knew well. The best thing she could do now was keep her mouth shut. It was the safest way to endure one of Simon's tirades, but she was too stubborn for her own good and her frustration won over her will.

Words tumbled from her tight lips before she could stop them. "If I'm so terrible, why don't ya just leave?"

"You ungrateful—" He slapped her hard enough to turn her sideways, but she kept to her feet. If he got her on the ground, he'd start kicking. "You want to know why I stay? Because God has seen fit to make me a modern-day Hosea. His plan for me was to marry a harlot. He knows I deserve so much better than you, and yet I endure. I am an example to show God's condemnation and great love for his people. I love you unconditionally, not because you deserve it, but because it is the burden I must bear. But you are a good-for-nothing heathen who must be refined by fire, and it is my duty to see to it."

He grabbed hold of her good arm and dragged her to the shed, where he shoved her backward against the wall. While he held her there, his hand went to her throat. "If you feed me one more egg from those chickens, I swear—"

"Clara?" A woman's voice came from behind. It was quiet but strong.

Clara blinked away the memory of her husband's cruel face. Her hand went to her throat to smooth away the sensation that had remained of Simon's rough fingers.

"You're up early," Clara said, her words choked with emotion. "You sleep okay?"

"Better than the last few nights. With all the provisions crammed in the bunker, it's always a tight fit for all three of us, but after escaping Julian, I don't think I would have slept at all if it wasn't for the safety of the hiding place."

Clara swiped a finger across her cheek to remove an offending tear before she turned to Eva. "Yeah, well, if it wasn't for those provisions, we'd be starving by next week." She pushed off the step. "I'll make breakfast. Escaping a madman and stopping a library bombing can work up an appetite."

"It's been a couple of days."

"And you didn't eat much last night. You need to keep your energy up."

"You making eggs, by any chance?"

Clara winced. "I'm afraid we don't have a lot of options. There's no room for complainers in this house."

"I'm not complaining. You want to hear something strange?"

"What?"

"I love eggs."

Clara pushed her lips together and walked past Eva into the house. "I didn't know lovin' eggs was so strange."

"Not for most people, but it turns out that before I lost my memory, I hated them."

"How do you know that?"

4

"Michael, this guy I used to work for who Julian invited to the house while I was there. He knew me pretty well and told me that before I lost my memory, I loved tennis and hated eggs."

"So that bump on your head made you all screwy and now you hate tennis and love eggs?"

"Haven't tried tennis yet."

Clara harrumphed. "My late husband liked eggs unless he hated them."

"Oh yeah?" Eva smiled. "Did he get a bump on the head too?"

"Nope. He just had very particular tastes that constantly changed. It was hard to keep up. Would you mind going to the bunker and grabbing me a couple cans of baked beans?"

"Sure. Is that all you need?"

"I've got everything else for now."

She forced a smile until Eva left the room, then leaned on the counter, taking several deep breaths. She should know better than to let her mind wander to the past. It did nothing but renew her pain and stir up fear. She had to focus on where she was today, because if she wasn't careful, she'd mess up any chance of having joy in her life.

Eva was the first person Clara had known to treat her with true kindness, and she'd nearly ruined it by allowing her son to tie Eva up and almost kill her. Now she found herself with a second chance. It was nothing short of a miracle that Eva, for whatever reason, was willing to put her trust in Clara again. And this time she wouldn't mess it up.

Eva returned to Clara's bedroom and looked down into the darkness below. The entrance to the underground bunker was hidden in Clara's closet and impossible to see if you didn't know what you were looking for. She wasn't lying to Clara about it being the only reason she could sleep at night, but it made her shudder to think that she was more comfortable huddled in hiding than sleeping in a regular bed. She wasn't normal with or without her memory, but she carried a deep anxiety that if her memories ever returned, she'd revert to the terrible person she was convinced she once was.

While she was leaning forward to get onto the ladder, a face appeared below and she jumped back before forcing her hands to relax from the fists that had clenched at her side, ready for a fight.

"Hey," Ben said as his head emerged from underground. "You okay? You look pale." His hair was messy from sleep but his eyes were bright.

"Sure, fine."

He climbed out of the hole. "Can't blame you for being tense. We won't be able to relax anytime soon, but we need to take advantage of this small reprieve while we can."

"Reprieve?" She shook her head. "I have these brief moments of normality when I forget how crazy my life has already been in my short memory. That's about all the reprieve I get."

"Did you get any sleep last night?"

"Yeah. I slept well."

"Really? 'Cause it doesn't look like it."

She pursed her lips. "That's because lack of sleep is not what's causing most of my exhaustion. It's not knowing what we're facing, or how to fight it, that I'm finding hard."

"Hey." He touched her arm. "We'll find a way to stop him."

"How? I can't remember anything and frankly, I don't want to if I can help it. Then there's the stuff we *do* know about. The bombs, the manipulation, the kidnapping…"

"That's a lot you've piled on your plate for this early in the morning. At this rate you won't have any room to fit Clara's breakfast."

"I know you think your humor is helpful, but mostly I find it annoying."

"It's better than focusing on things that are currently out of our control."

"Or it's a way of avoiding the inevitability of our failure to ultimately stop Julian."

"I think you're getting ahead of yourself. It'll be okay. If you want me to be serious, I can. I'm confident we can fight this."

"You say that like we're facing a bad health report and not a psychopath who has a massive head start on us and is determined to control a country."

Ben smiled and it caught Eva off guard. "That's not what I'm saying."

"Then what are you saying? You're so relaxed about the whole thing, and I can't understand how that's possible."

"When I was in the special forces, I had to lead teams into very dangerous situations and keep everyone calm throughout. If you can't keep your stress levels moderated, you put everyone in danger. As the leader, if I was relaxed, they were relaxed. It was the easiest way to get the best out of my guys."

"So now it's how you think you can get the best out of me?"

"I'm trying to help. Before you lost your memory, you were probably better at managing your anxiety. For now, what you have to remember is that we can't fix every problem at once. We can only take things one step at a time."

Ben didn't move away from the closet door and the untroubled countenance that he maintained as he stood there watching her reminded her of the first night they had been there when they'd almost kissed.

The air was suddenly hot. She pointed into the closet. "I need to get through there. Clara asked me to do some grocery shopping for her."

"Grocery shopping?"

"Yeah. She needs some supplies from the bunker."

"Oh. I'll get out of your way, then." But as she tried to slip past him, he stopped her. "Is something else bothering you?"

"Like what?" They were too close.

"I don't know. You just seem...tense all of a sudden."

Stepping back, she cleared her throat. "I'm fine. I just need to get through." The look he gave her sent a flush up her face and she focused on the ladder.

Thankfully, Ben turned his head and breathed deeply of the smells coming from the kitchen as he shifted out of her way. "Don't take too long. Smells like breakfast is ready."

"Yup." She scrambled into the hole.

"Don't forget. One step at a time." His voice echoed into the corridor as she hurried through the darkness.

He had a way of making her feel completely defenseless, vulnerable, and protected all at the same time. And even though she didn't fully trust herself with him, she did trust him with her life.

The aroma of frying bacon had followed her all the way down the hall causing her stomach to growl as she stepped into the large bunker. She pressed her hands on her hips and let out a sigh. The room was full of unmarked boxes. Her breakfast would be cold by the time she found the beans.

Beginning her search, she reminded herself that living here was not a long-term solution. She didn't like using up Clara's resources. If they survived this, she'd already decided she'd find a way to make it up to the woman who was somehow the closest thing she had to a mother figure in her life. A messed-up broken one who had almost participated in Eva's death, but one of a very small group who actually cared about her. It was messed up, but it was all she had.

She made her way through the boxes and crates, noting what was inside for later, and finally found what she was looking for in a box marked "Only Open in an Emergency" written in thick black marker. She opened it and found the beans she'd been looking for along with a stash of creamed corn.

When she returned to the kitchen, Ben was walking out the door. She waited until he was gone before making her presence known.

"Boy," Clara said. "That man can eat." She turned to take the cans from Eva. "Took you long enough. I thought maybe you got lost down there."

"I almost did. Just out of curiosity, did your husband hate baked beans and creamed corn?"

"He sure did. Those were the only two things he consistently despised." Then she added with a sneer, "Besides me, of course."

Eva started to smile until she saw the pained look on Clara's face. "At least he didn't write the same warning on you that he wrote on that box." She immediately regretted her words. She wasn't as good at humor as Ben.

"You'd be surprised." Clara rotated her arm around, stretching her shoulder.

"You okay?"

"Old injury is playing up. It gives me grief now and then, but nothing for you to worry about."

"What happened?"

"I used to be a top-level gymnast. Hurt it on a floor routine. That was the end of my career."

"Really?"

"No. But it makes for a better story than the truth."

Eva laughed even though she could guess at the real cause of the affliction. "Maybe, but I bet you have some other interesting stories to tell."

"Nope. There's not much depth to me."

"Well, one thing's for sure, whatever makes you you, keep doing that. You're exactly what we need."

Clara's mouth scrunched up as she fought emotion. "Don't think anyone has ever said somethin' so nice before. Don't reckon I deserve it."

"If you need me to tell you I forgive you for what you did, then I forgive you."

Clara grabbed an onion and started cutting even though there was a pile already cooking. She hunched her shoulders forward and focused on chopping. "Don't know how you can," she said under her breath, but Eva heard it.

"You make it pretty easy for me."

"How's that?"

"You know what you did was wrong."

"Well, sure."

"And you wouldn't do it again."

"Never. Not in a million years. I could be cut into a thousand pieces, but I'd never—"

"I get it. And you've proved my point."

Clara shook her head. "Go sit down. I'll bring you your breakfast."

Eva squeezed Clara's shoulder, digging her thumb into a sore spot before giving it a pat and moving to the table. She had the fork to her mouth as soon as the plate was set in front of her.

"I can't believe the FBI left you your chickens," Eva said after swallowing a mouthful.

"Don't know why," Clara said before sitting down at the table herself. "Only thing I can figure is that when they tramped around the property creating all kinds of commotion, the chickens ran and hid. I reckon those FBI agents didn't even know they were there. Smart chooks or stupid feds. I'm leaning toward the latter. A few days later I found Barry wandering the woods too."

"Barry?"

"Goat," Ben said from the door.

Eva looked up at him. "Barry, huh? How is it that the whole time I was here, I didn't know he had a name and yet you've been here a couple of days and you already know?"

Ben smirked and leaned against the doorframe. "I'm observant."

"They all have names," Clara said.

"You'll have to fill me in later."

Eva worked on devouring her breakfast while Clara and Ben talked about the hassles of looking after gardens.

Normal was Eva's new drug. It transported her to a different world for a few precious moments before she was forced to return to a reality that whispered of the suffering that was ahead.

"How do you keep the raccoons out?" Ben asked as Eva went to the sink to wash up. "They kept ruining my vegetables."

"They're good for target practice."

"Haven't tried that."

"Don't reckon there's much point in you learning to be a better gardener though."

"Why not?"

"Unless you two are here to play house, we've got

more important things to do. I get the impression we don't have much time to stop Julian."

Ben sighed. "I wanted us to have a break. But there are also complications."

"Such as?"

"We don't know what Julian has planned."

"Lynn will know," Eva said from the sink as she scrubbed at a dried bit of egg yolk stuck to the plate.

"Who?"

"Lynn. She knows about what's going on. She'll be able to give us more information." Eva turned from her work to look at Ben and Clara when they didn't respond. They were staring at her. "What?"

Ben spoke slowly. "Eva, who is Lynn?"

Chapter 2

JULIAN PULLED the car into the dirty lot. He was careful where he put his feet when he got out. This was the filthiest he'd seen it. Broken bottles and fast-food wrappers that had built up over the years decorated the edges of the barren parking area.

With a snarl of contempt, he made a call. "I thought you said you'd get this place cleaned up."

"Sorry, sir. Are you there now?"

"I am. You'd think people would have a little decency. It's no wonder the world has made a mess of itself."

"I'll make a call and get it done."

"Make sure it happens today." He hung up and picked his way across the mess to a low rusty railing that looked out over the city. It was a view he'd always admired. It had given him strength when he needed it. When plans didn't go his way, he could come up here and remind himself what it was all for. And that's what he needed today.

Everything had been going perfectly for him until that point. He had gotten Eva back. The man who had destroyed his facility a year earlier was in his grasp. And an explosion in a public library would begin the next phase of his plan.

He rubbed at his eyes when his thoughts muddled. It had only been a few days since Eva and Ben had escaped and made a mess, but every day since, he'd battled with a clouded mind. Sometimes it was so bad, it felt like he was losing his mind. But he wouldn't give in to it.

Blinking out at the horizon, he rubbed his eyes again when the scenery changed. The sky remained a clear blue, but the city had darkened as though the sun was hidden behind a cloud.

He squinted as the city rippled with what looked like waves of heat. Then there was fire, and he stepped back as flames twisted into faces that were somehow clear to see. When he blinked again, the city was gone, and all that was left was a pit of burning fire, boiling with bodies.

"Nice view."

The voice beside him sent him jumping sideways. He quickly hid the terror on his face when he saw who it was. "Michael. I'm sorry. I didn't hear you arrive."

"Sorry to startle you. Are you okay?"

"Fine. I was lost in thought, that's all. You found the place all right?"

"It was trickier than I expected. But judging by the garbage, others have found it quite easily."

"We're working on cleaning it up."

"But won't they come back?"

"Not after we erect a fence."

"Good." Michael crossed his arms and looked at the city. "You need to protect beauty."

The thing Julian liked most about Michael was not just his faithfulness to service. His greatest asset was that he never wavered. He'd done an excellent job enamoring Eva to him, and even though that hadn't worked out how they had anticipated, Michael still had a smile on his face.

"Thank you for meeting me here on such short notice. I hadn't expected to move ahead so quickly on this project, but after what happened—well, I'm reminded that we need to be vigilant and ready."

"I will say I'm intrigued meeting in this type of environment. If I didn't know you better, I'd be concerned you were about to kill me."

"Although it may appear to be a secrecy issue, this is not a clandestine meeting. However, I expect you to keep this place to yourself."

"I won't tell a soul."

"I also needed an excuse to get out of the house and clear my head." He breathed in deeply, then regretted it. "I used to love this place. I'll bring it back to its former glory."

"I take it I'm not here simply to reminisce about the good ol' days?"

Julian smiled. "No. I try to focus on the future. But that doesn't mean the past doesn't dig its thorns in now and then."

"It's unfortunate what's happened."

"How are you doing, by the way? I've been wanting to ask but didn't want to make you uncomfortable."

"Me? I'll be fine. There's no obstacle I haven't overcome yet."

"I know you were excited about kindling a connection with Eva."

"That's what you're worried about? Me and Eva?"

"You always liked her."

"I did, yes. But after what she's done, it's better things didn't go any further. Besides, there are plenty of other opportunities out there for me. I'm more concerned about the effect it's had on you."

"While I was hopeful for a different outcome, I've learned a valuable lesson. But I have other matters to consider. Like Ray, for example. How's he doing? You haven't given me an update on his arrest after his failed attempt at the library bombing. Have you been able to confirm that the police will not make any connection between him and us?"

"I was waiting to give you the full outcome until after his arraignment, but I've spoken to his lawyer. We have nothing to fear from him."

"You mean *our* lawyer."

Michael smirked. "Yes. Ray is very grateful that we've been so generous in recommending a good lawyer."

"He is one of the best. Still, it shouldn't have happened. I'm sorry to give you extra work."

"It wasn't your fault."

"It was. I mentioned the bombing to Ben. I was

trying to get information out of him, but I should have known better."

"You couldn't have."

"I trusted Eva too much."

"You couldn't have foreseen how she would react."

"I should have!" he shouted. "I'm sorry. It's been difficult and I have no one to blame but myself."

"I can't imagine what you must be going through right now. If there is anything I can do to help, please let me know."

"I will. Thank you for your concern."

"It was such an unfortunate time for her to regain her memory."

"That's the odd thing about it. I don't believe she has."

"You think that's possible? Why would she have turned on you like that?"

"I don't know, but the way she was talking, it sounded to me like she had no idea what was happening."

"Then why did she free Ben and escape with him?"

"The only thing that makes sense is that the trauma of seeing a man tied up and beaten broke something inside her. She'd suffered a lot. After everything that's happened, I believe she may have been scared."

Michael stuffed his hands into his pockets when a cool breeze picked up. "You don't think she was pretending?"

"She had no reason to. If she were really trying to escape, she would have left immediately, but she appeared unsure. Ben had to convince her. I only wish I had done a better job of convincing her to stay."

"Can I make a suggestion?"

"I'm all ears."

"If you locate her and still believe she has no memory, it might be best if I approach her. There could still be a chance to salvage this. When I came to your house to see her, my presence appeared to have a calming influence on her. If you recall, she was very taken with me."

"While I believe you are correct, and I appreciate your offer, we've gone past that."

"Julian—"

"No. I won't make the same mistake twice. I've got enough on my plate right now dealing with the naysayers who see this as an opportunity to discredit me."

"I'd heard whispers."

"We've already disposed of one or two troublemakers."

"I'm sorry to hear that. That could have only added to your frustrations."

"I stay focused on the positive. It helped us to weed out trouble. It saved us in the long run. But I can't deny that even with no memory, Eva is still against me." He flipped his hand in the air to dismiss the concerned frown on Michael's face. "The way things are coming along with Katy, I have no need for Eva."

"You can't really feel that way."

"It has nothing to do with how I feel. I was ready to

have her killed the first time, and that is where I am again. My mind is made up."

"I understand...But what if she contacts me?"

Julian laughed. "You really are an optimist. Or perhaps you like her more than you let on?"

"I like to expect the best out of life."

"I am confident she won't contact you, but if she does, do with her as you like. I have no more use for her. But promise me one thing."

"You've made me a generous offer. I'll do anything you ask."

"If you're lucky enough to get your hands on her, you must ensure she cannot interfere further with my plans. Kill her or lock her up, I don't care. But whatever you do, don't underestimate her."

"I won't."

"Good. Then, if you'd like to follow me, I'll show you why I've really brought you here."

"So there *is* more? Lead the way."

Julian waved his arm around the dirty lot. "As I said before, this will all be fenced off and cleaned up." He walked toward a clump of trees and underbrush. "There's another entrance, but I wanted you to experience it this way."

"I shouldn't have worn my good suit."

"I'll buy you another one. It will be worth it." He pushed through to a path that became visible once they were under the canopy of trees. "It's not far."

When they emerged out the other side, they encountered a barbed-wire fence surrounding a large low building with several giant satellite dishes on the top.

Michael reached toward the fence to link his fingers onto it, but Julian pulled him back. "It's electrified."

"Thanks for the warning." He looked along the fence line. "You wouldn't even know this was here."

Julian nodded appreciatively. "That's the point."

"Are you planning to buy this?"

"I already did."

Michael's eyebrows lifted. "What's it for?"

"What do you think?"

"It doesn't look big enough to be the hub of your new operation. Are you creating outposts?"

"It goes five stories underground."

Michael whistled. "Understated as usual."

"You know I don't like to draw attention."

"Okay, I'm impressed. You must be confident that the bill will pass."

"I know it will pass."

Michael put his hands on his hips and surveyed the property again. "When will it be operational?"

"Six months or less."

"That soon? Is there work going on already? It looks vacant."

"Yes, it does. The entry point is half a mile away with complete underground parking. I don't want anyone to know about what is going on in there except for those I've personally cleared. I've made the mistake of trusting the wrong people once and I won't do it again. I won't lose this building like I did that last one— what? I can see on your face you're dying to ask something."

"I'm sorry. I hate to bring her up again, but was Eva

ever informed about this place either before or after she lost her memory?"

"No, thankfully. She knew I was looking for a building, but I hadn't brought her here yet. Things hadn't progressed that far."

"That's a relief. I suppose it would have only meant extra precautions, but it would have been one more worry for you."

"No, but if she does somehow get her memory back, there is a lot of damage she could do to the Underwood Foundation. We'll need to remain vigilant either way."

Michael sighed. "Despite the risks you constantly manage, I'm glad you've settled here. This looks perfect. It is your future. From here, nothing will stop you. This is a powerful moment. From here, you will rule."

Julian took a deep, satisfied breath. "Indeed. It has been a dream for so long. To be standing in this place is certainly momentous."

Chapter 3

BEN WATCHED as the revelation of what Eva had said sunk in. She opened her mouth to respond, but no sound came out. She stood still for a minute, trying to process what had happened. Then she blinked, dropped the plate in the sink, and walked out the door without saying a word.

"What'd you think that was?" Clara whispered, leaning against the table so she could get a look at Eva outside.

"I have no idea."

"Do you think she got her memory back?"

"I don't think so, but I'm going to go find out."

Ben stood at the door giving Eva a moment before joining her on the porch. "You okay?"

"I don't know."

"But you've remembered something. Someone."

"No." She looked at Ben and pressed her lips together. "That's the thing. I have no idea who Lynn is or why I said her name. I was distracted washing the plates, and it slipped out."

"Okay, that's okay." He kept his tone soft. "When you thought of her, did you get any other impression besides a name? Does she work for Julian?"

"I don't—wait. No. She works at the White House."

"You sure?"

"You asked if I had any other impression. That's the impression I have. But I can't be certain whose side she's on."

"But you have some connection to her."

"I don't know." She walked down onto the grass. "I have no idea about any of it. She could be anyone. She could be my enemy."

"Is that the sense you get? I thought you said she could give us more information."

"I don't know!" she shouted and walked toward the woods, stopping in the middle of the yard. She turned back to Ben. "I'm sorry. I'm frustrated." She pushed her palm against her forehead. "I don't know what to think. I wish I knew more, but I don't."

"You can trust your instincts."

"How do you know?"

"Because I've experienced them firsthand, remember? You saved my life."

"So? That doesn't make me a good person."

He sighed. There was more going on under the surface than just Lynn. "It means we're on the same side."

"You can't know that for sure."

"I'm sure enough to trust you. You weren't on

Julian's side before you lost your memory, remember? The whole reason you have amnesia is because he tried to kill you."

"That doesn't mean I'm on the good side. What if I'm a darker version of Julian? What if I wanted to be in charge and my plan the whole time was to usurp him?"

"That doesn't make any sense."

"Why not?"

"What about all that scripture that you had memorized?"

"That could mean anything."

"Eva, come on. You know as well as I do that we're on the same side."

"You don't know that for certain."

"Yes, I do. I don't understand why you're fighting this so hard."

She focused on the forest. "Because I can't afford to be wrong."

"Even with no memory, you couldn't hide a part of yourself that was that dark. Unless you're pretending now."

She closed her eyes. "No. I'm not pretending." Her voice was so quiet, Ben almost didn't hear her.

"We don't have any other leads, so we need to focus on this woman Lynn and see if we can figure out who she is. You said she had more information. You can assume you must have been working with her to stop Julian. If we can find her, there might be a plan already in motion."

"We can go with that theory, but even if she is safe, we have no way to find her."

"Can you remember a last name?"

"No."

"What about the keypad?"

"What?"

"The keypad you unlocked when you found me at Julian's."

"What about it?"

"You said you let your fingers punch the right numbers into a keypad by muscle memory. Maybe you can do that with a phone number."

Eva scoffed. "That's a long shot. A very long shot. You're assuming I have a number memorized for her in the first place."

"I doubt you would have written it down anywhere."

"What if it doesn't work?"

"Then it doesn't work. But we can at least try. You wanted a next step. This is better than anything else I can think of."

Eva scrubbed a hand across her mouth. "What if I *do* get through to her? What do I say?"

"That's what you're worried about?"

Her head dropped. "I don't know what I'm worried about."

"Hey, we're all in this together. You're not alone. We'll figure it out as we go. Together."

"But you're not the one who everyone's hopes are pinned on. You're not the one who should be able to fix this if your brain was functioning properly."

"No one expects you to fix this on your own."

"But this is more my fault than yours."

"What does that mean?"

"I worked with Julian. I helped him get to where he is."

"Eva, I'm sorry, but none of this is your fault. The one responsible is Julian and anyone who is actively helping him *now*. You have got to stop going around in circles with guilt. That won't help anyone, especially you. If you don't want to do anything, fine. I won't force you, but you're letting your self-condemnation stop you from doing anything. Doing nothing means Julian has no one to stop him."

Eva's head sagged to the ground. "I don't want to make another mistake."

"Then let this one be my mistake. If it backfires on us, that's on me. But I still think it's worth trying."

Eva looked back at the house and winced. "Okay. But I don't know how we're going to call her. Clara doesn't have a phone."

"I bet she does."

"Trust me."

"You might be surprised."

"I'm telling you, she doesn't."

"We'll see."

Ben ran back to the house, jamming his hands on the doorframe to stop his momentum. "Hey."

Clara jumped. "Goodness gracious. You scared the livin' daylights outa me."

"Sorry."

"Is Eva okay?"

"She's fine. You don't have a burner phone around here by any chance?"

"What for?"

"She's going to try to call Lynn. See if the number is somewhere in her memory."

Clara stood. "Always be prepared." She disappeared down the hall as Eva walked through the door.

"Where's she going?" She sat at the table like she was exhausted.

"To get a phone."

"You're kidding."

"Nope."

Clara returned holding a package up in the air. "One burner phone. Untraceable. You're welcome." She set it on the table.

When Eva didn't reach for it, Ben picked it up and ripped it open. "Remember, there's no pressure. Just try it." He set up the phone and checked to make sure there was enough charge before putting it back in front of Eva.

"How exactly does this work?" Clara asked as Eva picked up the phone and turned it around in her hands. "I take it we've all agreed that Lynn is a real person?"

"Who knows," Eva said.

"And her phone number is hidden somewhere in your head?"

"Who knows."

Ben cleared his throat. "We're hoping. Eva punched in a number she didn't remember to unlock a door at Julian's. She's going to try that again with Lynn's number."

"Interesting."

Eva sighed, ran her finger over the numbers, then held her breath and closed her eyes.

"What's wrong?" Ben asked.

"Nothing. I need—If the number is locked in my head, then it'll be like a word that's on the tip of my tongue. I can't overthink it. If it's in there, I have to get my brain out of the way."

She puffed out her cheeks, then stretched her neck from one side to the other.

Her fingers dragged across the keys before she spun her hand around so her thumb could press the buttons more naturally.

"Here goes nothing." She dialed a number, but it came back as disconnected.

"Lynn's number is disconnected?" Clara said.

"I don't know. I didn't get the code for the door right the first time. I had to try a couple of times. But what if it is?" She looked at Ben.

"Try it again," he said.

"If she knew I'd gone back to Julian, she may have gotten rid of the number."

"Maybe, but we can't give up yet."

Eva clenched her teeth, but lifted the phone again. The next number she tried wasn't even a number. She tried again, and a man answered.

"Hello?"

"Hi, it's Eva—I mean—" She winced. "I'm looking for Lynn. Is she there?"

"No. I'm sorry. You must have the wrong number."

"Okay. Sorry to bother you." She hung up and

dropped the phone on the table. "I shouldn't have said my name. I got flustered. I should have been better prepared."

"It's fine. It was a wrong number. He has no idea who you are."

"This won't work."

"Eva, come on. You've dialed three numbers. How many times did it take you to get the door lock?"

"This is different. It didn't matter if I got through that door. I was just trying it."

"Actually, it mattered a great deal that you got through that door."

"Yeah, but I didn't know that when I was trying. I can't do this when I'm stressed."

"Then relax."

She scowled. "Easy for you to say. You're not the one hunting for a number that may be nonexistent."

"You can't give up yet."

Eva stared up at the ceiling. With so much riding on this, they were all on edge, but she looked like she wanted to put her hand through the wall.

"You can do this." Ben walked behind her. "Here." He rubbed her shoulders. "Does this help?"

"Not really." She shrugged him off. "Just give me a second."

After letting out a slow deep breath, she dialed again. The number went to the voice mail of a mobile mechanic. The next two times people answered, but no one knew anyone named Lynn.

She avoided contact with everyone in the room and

her posture curved inward after every call. She dialed again and was told it was a wrong number.

"It won't work," she said when she hung up. "I can't do it. I don't know the number."

"You've barely tried," Ben said.

"You want to call Lynn so badly, then you do it." She threw the phone at him and raced out the door.

"That was stupid," Clara said with a snort.

"Go easy on her. She's stressed."

"I don't mean her, ya idjit. Have a little compassion."

"Me have compassion? All I've done is try to help her. You're the one who tied her up——"

"You know nothin' about it. If Eva's willing to forgive me, that's all I need. If you don't like it, you're free to go."

"I'm sorry. I shouldn't have said that. I'm just frustrated."

"Aren't we all? That's no excuse," she grumbled and left the room.

Ben pushed his fingers through his hair and got up from the table. God had placed them all in an impossible scenario. But it wouldn't be the first time. And as much as Ben would like to deny his faithfulness for the sake of being right, he knew God would come through somehow. It may not come as fast as they wanted, and it may not be how they expected, but it would come.

Chapter 4

JULIAN PAUSED when he reached the closed door. His outing with Michael had done little to calm him. He'd enjoyed his time showing off his new facility, but stepping back into his house reminded him of what he'd lost.

Maybe it was his pride that had caused the fall. But his pride had never failed him before. If Tyler weren't such an excellent employee, he would have murdered him just to let out his frustration. But he couldn't let his losses get to him. Every great man had faced powerful adversaries and overcome them. He had done so in the past and he would do the same again.

He filled his lungs to dispel the memories and settle himself before he entered the room.

With a forced smile on his face, he opened the door to the living room. Katy, his eight-year-old replacement for Eva, sat in the middle of the floor on a multicolored rug with her legs crossed and eyes closed. Mrs. Beaman stood to the side, observing. She looked up when Julian entered and put a finger to her lips before focusing back on the girl.

Julian walked silently to the closest chair and sat watching while Katy's head lolled from one side to the other. Every now and then, her face scrunched into a snarl before a serene smile took its place.

Finally, she opened her eyes. They were dark and mischievous for a moment when they settled on Julian, but when she jumped off the floor, a wide grin took the place of a malevolent squint. The young girl had returned.

"Uncle Julian!" She gave him a high five, then stepped back. "I didn't know you were coming today."

"I've had a rough day. I needed some cheering up."

"I know. You thought everything would be hunky-dory, and it's not."

Her head tipped sideways and Julian looked at Bea, who lifted her eyebrows, then bent over to pick up the rug Katy had been sitting on. "Don't look at me. I didn't tell her anything."

Julian took Katy's hand. "No, everything is not hunky-dory. The first thing I thought was that I needed to visit my star pupil. You always make me smile."

"Can I do anything to help?"

"You absolutely can. You can tell me about all the interesting things you've been learning."

She scrunched up her face. "How's that supposed to help?"

"It helps by getting my mind off the things I can't currently control and cheers me up because I always like to hear about what you're doing. What is it you were doing on the floor when I came in?"

"Bea has been teaching me about meditation."

"I thought that's what you were doing. How's it going?"

"I made a new friend."

"During your meditation?"

"Yep. He always visits me when I'm inside my mind."

Julian looked at Bea again. She was sitting, focused intently on the magazine in front of her. He knew she was listening, but she obviously preferred to stay out of it at this point. That was fine. He needed to speak to her alone about this, anyway.

"A friend, huh?" Most of the students took part in some form of meditation. It aided them in molding the children. It was easier to introduce new ideas during times of reflection, but he couldn't remember anyone making a friend while in a meditative state.

"And who might this friend be?"

"His name is Harold. He said he knows you."

"Oh he does, does he? I can't say I know him."

"He says you do. He's the one that told me what happened. He said when you came to see me, I should remind you about him."

"The only Harold I know of is my great-great-grandfather, and he died before I was born."

"Katy," Bea interrupted, "I'd like to speak to Julian for a moment. Why don't you go into the kitchen and get yourself a snack?"

"Ooh," she whined. "But I'm supposed to tell him about Harold."

"I'm perfectly capable of telling him."

"But I promised." She cut the whine off when Bea gave her a look that said she was about to cross a line. Katy's head dropped. "Fine. But I'm telling Harold."

"Are you threatening me?" The brightness in Bea's voice did not hide the warning.

"No."

"Good, because I'm sure he is well aware of what has transpired and will not be impressed. Now off you go."

Julian took Katy's hand. "Don't worry. I'll make some more time for you. I promise."

"Okay." She trudged out of the room.

"I'm sorry you had to see that," Bea said when Katy was gone. "She can be difficult to handle at times and needs a firm hand."

"No need to apologize. I'm very happy with how well she's coming along. We can't forget she is only a child."

"True, although you shouldn't let her age fool you. She is well advanced for her years. She is miles ahead of the others in many areas, including what you just saw."

"The meditation."

"Yes. Your timing was perfect. I'm glad you could observe her."

"I observed *her*, but not this friend she spoke about."

"Harold."

"Did you know about him?"

"Yes. That's the most exciting part."

"Exciting is probably not the word I would use for an imaginary friend."

"It would be rather ordinary if Harold were pretend. But I can assure you, he is not. It's what I wanted to talk to you about." Bea folded her hands in her lap. "I knew when we first brought her in. She's very open. Much more than any of the others."

"More than Eva?"

Bea pursed her lips. "Eva was impressive in a lot of ways, but meditation was never her strength. No matter what I did, her mind remained closed."

"I don't remember you ever mentioning it."

"That's because I never did. There was no point. She had so many other abilities and you were very fond of her, so I left it alone."

"But? I can see on your face that there is a 'but.'"

"But it caused me a great deal of frustration over the years."

"Why should it?"

"If I'm honest with you, Julian, I wasn't surprised when she turned on you. A corner of her mind had been infiltrated by someone or something else. A darkness was inside her that wouldn't allow the light to shine in. I tried very hard, but after a great deal of effort, I finally gave up."

Julian shook his head. "She complied with everything. I can't believe she wouldn't participate in the meditations."

"She did participate. But I always felt she was playing a part and not really engaging with it as the others have."

Julian had always known that Bea never took to Eva as well as he did, and he had always wondered why. Now he knew.

"You've obviously found Katy to be much more open."

"Very much. I could see it from the beginning, so I asked her about her experience before coming to stay with us. As it turned out, her mother had similar beliefs."

"I remember reading about that in one of the reports. So, do you do things differently with Katy than you do the others?"

"Yes."

"In what way?"

"With the other children, we do the basics. Enough to clear their minds of any hindrances. With Katy, I go deeper."

"Why not treat everyone the same? Do you think it's possible that there are others who share Katy's gifts that you haven't picked up on?"

"Perhaps, but we can't risk it. You have handpicked these kids. If we aren't careful, we could lose some of them. I don't want that to happen."

Julian chose his words carefully. He trusted Bea. She'd been a part of his life since childhood and she did wonderful work with the training, but he was not as extreme in his beliefs as she was when it came to the more spiritual aspects of the training. "Lose them how?"

"Do you recall the incident with a young man named Kyle several years ago?"

"He's the boy who started the fire?"

"Correct."

"You believe that was from meditation practices?"

"I do. I worked with him myself on occasion. He was promising, but I should have seen the signs."

"And you still think it's a good idea to do the same with Katy? You believe that's wise?"

"Like I said. Katy's different."

"I hope you're right because I think she could be the one to take over from me, and I'd hate to lose her to another fire."

"I couldn't agree more."

"Lucky for you, I found one you like."

"It isn't luck, Julian. She was destined for this time. As terrible as it was to lose Eva—twice, it has opened the way for Katy."

"You think it was a mistake for me to give her a second chance?"

"It's easy to recognize mistakes when we look backward. You did what you felt was best. I believe your biggest downfall was trusting in your emotion beyond what you should have."

"I wanted her back so bad I misread the signs?"

"Not necessarily. She had the potential to return, but even you knew it would be risky. I *do* wonder if she were anyone else, would you have still given her a second chance?"

"I doubt it."

"At least you're a realist. But there is no point being despondent about the past. We have a future to look forward to."

"You're right. And you still haven't told me about

this new friend of Katy's. Apparently he knows me, but I'm not sure how I would have met him. You never taught me about going deeper."

Bea smiled. "You don't remember, but you did. I was very young then, but my sole purpose in being there was to show you the truth."

"My father hired you to be my nurse."

"He did, but that wasn't why I accepted the work."

"You never told me this."

"No, it hasn't been the right time until now. I've been waiting for a sign, and I believe Katy is that sign."

"The right time for what?"

"In a way, I wasn't hired by your father. I was hired by your great-great-grandfather."

Julian scoffed. "Do you know how old that would make you?" He was dubious about her claim, but intrigued. His grandfather had told him of some of the more unconventional things Harold had been involved in. Julian had never been interested in devil worship, but from what he understood, Harold Underwood considered himself to be a servant of the entity. Julian preferred to rule on his own terms. Why serve a spirit when he could serve himself and those he led?

"I never knew Harold while he was alive," Bea said.

"Are you saying you speak to the dead?"

"More like the dead speak to me. Harold initiated our contact. He wanted to communicate with you because he saw something special in you. Your father and grandfather were not good candidates. But he was very excited about you. He just hadn't been able to speak to you about it."

"Why?"

"Your father was a rather rigid man who saw things in black and white. Some of that has rubbed off on you."

"That is true."

"I was there to show you another way."

"I do remember when you first began working for the family, we played those odd games. Although I found the chants to be tedious. And I certainly don't ever remember meeting my great-great-grandfather."

"I know you don't. But he had a big impact on you at that time."

"Are you saying I've forgotten?"

Bea sighed. "I've known you most of your life. You and Harold share a lot of similarities, but the traits you share with your father are unfortunate."

"Seeing things in black and white is a weakness?"

"It can be at times. Also, you seek power for selfish gain."

"That's not entirely true. I do want power, yes, but I also want humanity to prosper."

"You tell yourself that in your more generous moments, but deep down, you want to rule. You want to be king for the sake of it. There's nothing wrong with that, but there is something else inside you. A nature that transcends this lifetime. There is a seed that has been planted there and it is time to water it. You've spoken to me often of leaving a legacy. You believe that you have the answers mankind is striving to discover, but you are oblivious to where that motivation comes from.

You are unaware of the one who began the legacy in the first place."

"Are you saying my inspiration comes from Harold?"

"Him and the one whom he served."

Julian rubbed a hand across his mouth. "I appreciate what you're trying to do here, but I'm not interested in devil worship. I don't like the idea of drinking blood."

Bea's laugh was sprinkled with amusement. "I have never drunk anyone's blood."

"But you worship the devil."

"If you want to call him that. But he's not who you assume him to be. Asmodeus is not who you see represented in the movies. You would likely be surprised at the people who have committed themselves to his service. Ordinary people. People with great power and influence."

"Perhaps, but I'm not interested." He stood. "If you want Katy to believe she's friends with my great-great-grandfather, I'm fine with that as long as he doesn't convince her to set fire to my house." He turned to leave.

"Do you really believe that everything you've accomplished, you've done without the aid of a higher power?"

He'd always valued Bea for her candor. She had a way of turning truth so he could see it from a different angle. He didn't always agree with her, but he'd never dismissed her. Today, however, she'd hit a nerve. When his luck was running high, he had wondered about mystical powers at work, but once his luck turned, he had dismissed it. It was foolishness.

"I've been surprised by outcomes of late, yes. Some extraordinary things have occurred recently. But if this —what did you call him?"

"Asmodeus."

"Right. Asmodeus. If he wants to take responsibility for the good things, then he has to take responsibility for the bad as well. Why hand Eva over to me only to steal her away again?"

"I have a theory."

"You don't know for certain?"

"I've been doing this long enough to feel confident of my assessment."

"Okay. I trust you. What are your thoughts?"

"He's disciplining you for ignoring his favor."

"I've been on this path for most of my life and this is only coming up now?"

"Time is growing short. We are reaching the end."

Julian couldn't ignore the thrill that rocketed through him at the thought that he was nearing his goal. "I knew it. I knew I was close." Exhilaration pumped through his body. "I could feel it."

"Beware, Julian. Harold was the architect of this work that you do. If you wish to see it completed, you must remember."

"Remember what?"

"From your childhood."

"You believe that I was contacted by my dead ancestor?"

"I am certain of it. Harold knew you had what it would take to complete the work he began. Katy's the same."

"But not Eva."

Bea's face darkened. "You need to forget about her."

"I only want to understand. She's my daughter."

"I don't know what else to say about it. She wasn't open."

"I haven't been open and I've done just fine. Why not her?"

Bea's face bunched up in irritation. "She was different. There was something inside of her."

"What?"

"I don't know. Just that it was a darkness we could never break through."

"Did Asmodeus know?"

"Of course he did," Bea snapped. "He knows all."

"And what about Ben Waite? Does Asmodeus have anything to say about him?"

"Why don't you ask him yourself?"

"You're persistent."

"I only want what's best for you."

Julian sat down beside her. "You know I want to succeed more than anything. But these ideas of yours... they're hard to take."

"You say you want to succeed and yet you are unwilling to do what is required. You can't win these battles on your own. You need his help."

What could it hurt to indulge? "Okay, Bea. What do I need to do?"

A smile strained for release on her face, but she kept it in check. "For now, all you have to do is remember. The rest will follow."

"How do I remember?"

"Do you trust me?"

Julian grinned. "Those words alone are troubling."

"You have nothing to be concerned about. I never harmed you as a boy, did I? But I need you to put yourself into my hands once again."

"Okay, let's get this over with."

"Good. Lay your head back and close your eyes."

Julian did as he was asked.

Her fingernail dragged lightly across his forehead, then she took his hand and began drawing shapes on his palm with her finger.

It had been a long day, and he was tired. The fatigue wormed into the back of his eyes and dragged him into sleep. It would irritate Bea that he fell asleep, but he was too weary to resist.

Chapter 5

BEN ROSE FROM THE TABLE. Eva would need to stop running out of the house every time things got difficult, but he was also too used to being on his own and had to remember to be more careful with the people around him. He couldn't be stubborn with Eva, pushing his way as the right one.

He went outside and found her at the side of the house, using the doorframe of the shed to do chin-ups.

"You retained some of your fitness, I see?"

She ignored him.

"Eva, come on. I know I could have handled that better. I shouldn't have pushed you to make all those calls if you weren't ready."

"Twelve…thirteen…fourteen."

"I know this is hard, but you can't ignore me. I know I made it harder on you. I'm sorry."

She dropped to the ground. "Don't do that."

"Do what?"

"Apologize. There's no reason to."

"Then why'd you throw the phone at me and run off?"

"Because I was mad, but not at you. I can't afford to be useless."

"You're not useless."

She wiped sweat off her forehead with the back of her wrist. "I don't know why you think there's any point trying to make me feel better. You're wasting your time."

"I'm not trying to make you feel better—okay, I am, but I also happen to believe the words that I say. You're as important to all of this as any of us are. Probably more so."

"That's exactly my point. I'm the only one who has any intel on Julian and it's locked deep inside my head where I can't reach it. It's like the universe is trying to keep us from stopping him. You sure God really wants us to do the job? Because he isn't making it easy."

"God's not one to make everything in our lives easy. But one thing I know is that he's always right."

"You've found that every time?"

"Every single time. It's irritating."

She hid her laugh by grabbing hold of the door again and pulling herself up.

"Stop it," he said, grabbing the waist of her pants and yanking her back to the ground. "You're allowed to smile now and then."

"I like being angry. It suits me."

Ben made a face. "Not really. Your smile is much nicer than your scowl. Trust me. I'm the one who has to look at it."

"But my scowl is better for training. I'm out of shape."

"How do you know? You look pretty fit to me."

"Watch." She walked over to a knife sticking in the fence and pulled it out.

"You're not going to throw that at me, are you?"

"Wouldn't matter if I did," she said, walking back to stand next to him.

"I would have to disagree."

"Not if I threw it and missed."

"You're not planning on testing that theory, are you?"

"See that dark spot where I pulled it out?"

"Yeah."

She aimed, then threw the knife. It stuck an inch to the side of where she indicated. "See?"

He crossed his arms. "I'm not sure what I'm looking for here. That was a good throw. If I was standing there, I'd have a knife stuck in me right now."

"But I didn't hit the target."

"Most people wouldn't even be able to hit the post."

"I'm not most people."

"No, you're not. Like I said, that was a good throw."

"Really?" She stomped to the fence to fetch the knife, then went back and slapped it into his hand.

"What do you want me to do with this?" He threw it up in the air where it spun several times, then he caught the handle.

"Cute. Now throw it."

"Are you trying to prove something?"

"Just throw it."

"If you insist."

"I do."

He threw the knife. It hit the mark.

"See?" she said.

"Yeah, but I'm good with a knife."

"So am I."

"Just not as good as me." He grinned, then cowered in imaginary alarm when she glowered at him. "Those daggers you're throwing with your eyes are pretty accurate."

"I should be able to throw as well as you."

"How do you even know that? Maybe knives weren't your strong suit."

"They were. I'm familiar with knives. I can judge the weight by looking at it. Besides, I can feel it in my bones."

"*Okay, Clara.* I don't know what you're worried about. You weren't far off."

"I should be better."

"You're rusty. You need a bit more practice, that's all."

"Maybe. Or maybe I'm incapable of doing anything useful."

Ben sighed. "Show me what else you can do."

"Like what?"

"I don't know. What can you *feel in your bones*?"

She looked around, trying to let something come to mind, then she focused back in on Ben. "Hit me."

"What?"

She moved into a wider stance and bent her legs. "Hit me."

"I'm not going to hit you."

"You won't. But you can try."

"Oh okay. I see how it's going to be. You're nasty when you're in training." Last time they'd done this, she attacked him in the store when he tried to get a bottle of bleach for her. He had been impressed with her skill then, but she was no match for him. He'd have to be careful with her.

She winked at him, and he went in with a slow left hook. She dodged, grabbed his arm, and tripped him backward, sending him to the ground.

He laid there a second, looking up at her. "That was uncalled for."

"That's what you get for going easy on me. Come on, I need to know where I'm at with my training. You need to show me my weaknesses, and you can't do that when you're pulling punches."

"Okay, but you asked for it."

"I forgive you in advance. Now let's go."

Ben got up and paced in front of her for a few steps before jumping forward. But when she reacted to his advance, he twisted sideways and wrapped his arm around her waist, swinging her around and dropping her to the ground where he pinned her. "You're not making—"

She punched him in the stomach, then got a knee in and flipped him over, holding his arms down.

He didn't fight back. "You know I could throw you off me right now. You haven't got the weight to hold me down."

"I am aware of that." She blew hair out of her face.

"Normally I'd be mangling that pretty mug of yours right now."

"Aw, you think I'm pretty?"

"You really are asking for it, you know that?"

"Then hit me. If you think you can."

She let go of his arm to do as he said, but he'd anticipated her reaction. When he caught her arm, he flipped her over. She was back under him, and this time he made sure she didn't have any limbs free.

"Never go for a punch when you're on top of someone bigger than you."

"That was a little unfair. I gave you time to think."

"The outcome would have been the same."

"I did the same thing with Franky, except I didn't hesitate to pummel him while I had him down. It worked fine."

"But you would have caught Franky off guard. He wasn't aware of what you were capable of and he's not trained like I am, or the way Julian's guys are."

"I know that. Are you going to let me up?"

"Actually, I—" He was about to make a witty comment when he realized how much he really did not want to let go. He swung off her. "Sorry. I mean, I'm not sorry because we aren't apologizing anymore."

"Right." She sat up and pulled her knees up, wrapping her arms around them. "I guess I'm rusty with all of my fighting skills too. I can remember fighting them, you know."

"Fighting who?"

"Julian's guys. The night I fell in the river, I can remember someone tackling me."

"But you got free?"

"Yeah."

"So somewhere in there is hidden more skill."

"Somewhere. I just don't have it right now. May never get it back."

"You're still better than most."

"But that won't be good enough, will it? What do you think I should have done when I got you down? What do I do if it's not you?"

"If you have the chance to run, you run."

"What if I don't want to run?"

"Run anyway. You don't have the skill to fight back right now. Not against those guys."

"And if running isn't an option?"

He let out a breath and searched the lawn next to him. When he found a large blade of grass, he pulled it from the ground. "If you can't run, you stay on your feet." He put the grass between his thumbs and blew through the thin hole, making it squeak. "If you can get in a kick or two before your opponent can get up, do that. If you can get in enough kicks, you might get lucky and he won't be able to get back up. But Julian's guys... you'll have to be the one who's faster 'cause you won't be stronger." He whistled through the grass again. "I trained with a few of them. I know how good they are."

"I was wondering how you got involved with Julian in the first place. He never hires outsiders for the position that you had."

"I didn't understand back then, but it was a miracle. I was right where God wanted me to be."

"You didn't know that at the time?"

"No. I was too lost." Ben shook his head. "Julian has a knack for recognizing a person when they're most vulnerable and he knows how to spin a good tale."

"I can't remember him from before, but even the short time I was with him recently, it is so clear to me now when I think back over it. After he brought me home from the hospital, he told me everything I wanted to hear. I think I could have seen it if I hadn't been so scared."

"But you were exactly where God needed you to be. I know things aren't great, but imagine if anything had been different."

"I know. It just makes me sick to think about what he does. How he gets inside your head. I trusted him. I believed he cared about me."

Ben flicked the grass onto the ground. "He probably thinks he does care about you. That's what's so disturbing about all of this."

"But he tried to have me killed. He'd kill me now if he were here."

"He'd see it as a necessary sacrifice."

"That's ridiculous."

"But it's how he is. Trust me. If he had succeeded in killing you, he'd have been broken up about it."

"That can't be true."

"Why not?"

"Because Julian only cares about himself."

"I'm sure he does."

"So how would my death affect him at all besides celebration? He's a narcissistic—" She grunted in frustration. "I hate him so much and I barely know him."

Ben got to his feet. "We should probably stop talking about it. I don't think it will do either of us any good."

"But it's always there, isn't it? We can't completely ignore it." She stood and brushed her pants off. "I have these moments where I can forget it all for a fraction of a second. There is a part of me that wants to walk away and pretend like it's not real, but I can't."

"At least you had a few days of peace when you didn't know anything was going on."

"When?"

"After I rescued you from here. You went home with Julian and you were safe for a time."

"I never felt okay though. The whole time I was there, I was afraid. Not of Julian, but I couldn't escape this feeling like something was out to get me. The only time I was able to truly relax was when Michael—I couldn't really relax."

"What?"

"Nothing."

"Who's Michael?"

"No one. Just a guy who works for my dad."

"And he helped you relax?"

"No, I just—I forgot about my fear for a little while."

"How'd he do that? Maybe I can help."

"No! No, forget it. It doesn't matter."

"Your face is red. I take it Michael is charming?"

"Yes. Exactly. So you have no hope."

"Ouch. So you're saying he distracted you by hitting on you? You think it would help your mood if I flirted with you?"

"No. Now stop embarrassing me. You can stick to your fighting skills. That's plenty."

"Hey, I am a man of many talents."

"I'm sure you are."

"Here." He bent down and plucked a wide piece of grass. "Put this between your thumbs."

She crossed her arms. "Why?"

"Apparently, I'm not charming, so I'll have to find other ways to make you feel better."

"How is that going to make me feel better?"

"Trust me. Come on. Take it."

Eva was happy about the change in subject. She hadn't meant to bring up Michael. His name slipped out before she thought better of it. So even though she tsked like she thought playing with a piece of grass was ridiculous, she still took it and secured it between her thumbs.

"Now," Ben said after checking she had it right, "blow through your thumbs like you saw me do before."

She blew, but no sound came out. "You gave me a broken one."

Ben chuckled. "It's not broken." He took her hands and tightened the grass so it was more rigid. "Hold it tight, right where it is, and try again."

She glared at him, but blew again, eliciting a humming squeak.

Ben adjusted her hands more. "Give it another try."

She did and got a clearer sound. "Now what?"

"That's it. You did it. Congratulations."

"And this was supposed to make me feel better?"

"Did it work?"

It did. "Maybe a little. But don't get a big head about it."

"Don't worry. You make that impossible for me."

"Good."

"You know, there's also a lesson there."

"Oh great."

He shook his head. "You're a real piece of work when you're in a mood."

He was right. She wasn't giving him an inch, but she couldn't afford to. The only way she knew to protect herself from him was to keep up a thorny pretense. But she didn't want to push him away either. "Sorry. What's the lesson?"

"You want things to be easy, but life is never about easy. No one ever gets to a point in their life where it all makes sense and they've got everything together."

"First of all, that is not true. I don't want life to be easy, I just want a break from the awfulness that we're facing. Second, what in the world does that have to do with making grass squeak?"

"It's the tension. If you want to get the most out of life, there has to be tension. That grass makes no sound without pressure and tension."

Ben looked so earnest about gaining insight from a blade of grass that Eva started laughing and couldn't stop. "I'm sorry," she said when she caught her breath. "I'm over-stressed, but really, that is the worst object lesson I have ever heard in my life."

"Is that so? And how many object lessons can you remember hearing in your life?"

"You always gotta take the cheap shot. Using my memory against me is just plain lazy. And besides, that's not the point."

"I thought it was a pretty good lesson for something I made up on the spot."

"It would have been better if the grass didn't make the worst noise ever. The last thing I want in my life is tension, if that's the result."

"You don't think it's cool making music with a piece of grass?"

"That was not music."

He smiled. "But you do feel better."

She couldn't understand why he bothered trying to cheer her up. But she was glad he did. "I've got to admit, you find unusual ways to take my mind off things."

"Better than Michael?"

She laughed. "Will it help your ego if I say yes?"

"Absolutely."

"Then, yes."

He lifted his arms in the air in victory. "My life is complete."

Chapter 6

WAVES OF FIRE washed over Julian's body as his mind drifted to sleep. He opened his eyes in a confused panic, but all he could see was fog. Fog that burned.

He turned to his left, where the fog was lighter. Then ran to try to escape the fog but found he had no legs to run with. He looked down but saw nothing. Only the burning fog that scorched a body that didn't exist. He opened his mouth to cry out, but he had no mouth.

A hum rumbled the air. The vibration entered his mind and shook him. The pounding increased until the throbbing became worse than the burn. His mind screamed, but the pain didn't lift.

The surrounding fog brightened until his eyes hurt. When he tried to close them, he found he had no eyelids. He was in hell with no escape.

The only way out is to give in.

The thought pierced through the stupor of agony, but he resisted. The only way he knew how to survive was to resist. To fight until it was over. But what if it never ended?

Give in.

He tried to scream again, but the hopelessness intensified. He was powerless.

There's only one way out.

He couldn't take it. It was too much. Death would be a better option than enduring the pain any longer, but he knew somehow that death would not come to him.

He let go. Stopped fighting.

He gave in, then jumped up from the couch and out of his dream, choking for breath.

Spinning around, he searched the room for Bea, but she wasn't there. Then his legs gave out, and he fell to the floor.

"Bea," he croaked out. "What have you done to me?"

He pushed himself back against the couch and sat up, the dream sliding from him into oblivion.

The door opened and Bea entered the room, a friendly smile on her face.

"Bea, where did you go? Why weren't you here?" He wiped sweat from his face.

"I gave you the privacy you required."

"What happened to me?"

"What *did* happen to you?"

The innocence in the question and the tone of her voice infuriated him, but he had little strength to defend himself. "Don't act like you don't know. I—" But it was gone. He had the sense of something. He knew he was hurt, or afraid, or—what? He couldn't remember anything. "I thought—"

"You thought what?"

"I don't know."

"Was it bad?"

"I don't know."

She lifted an eyebrow. "But what do you remember?"

"I can't remember any—"

"Not the dream. Think back."

He pushed up from the floor and got up to the couch. Bea had seen him at his worst over the years, but he didn't like anyone to see him this weak. "I don't remember anything."

"Try."

Julian was frustrated. He might not remember the dream, but there was something. He wasn't this upset for no reason. "So whatever happened to me did something?"

"It was worth it. Trust me. What can you remember?"

He still had a sense of powerlessness he couldn't shake and would have preferred to be left alone to recover. But the only way he'd get rid of Bea would be to satisfy her that something had happened. Then he could leave this entire episode behind him. He should have left her to her devil worship. If he had known the outcome, he never would have agreed. He should have trusted himself more instead of looking to others to help him. He'd dealt with worse situations on his own. Now he'd deal with this one too.

To appease Bea, he took a breath and thought back to when he was a boy. A memory surfaced. One he hadn't thought of in a long time. "I remember words we'd repeat into the mirror. I thought it was nothing."

"What else?"

The image of a man. "That night in my dreams. A man stood at the bottom of my bed."

"You believe you were dreaming?"

"I thought I was at the time. Are you saying someone was there?" But he knew the answer even as he asked the question. The painting that he now had hanging in his study of his great-great-grandfather, it had been hanging in his father's library when he was a boy. He knew what Harold looked like. It was the same man. "Harold."

"Yes. Very good. Do you remember what he said to you?"

Something in his mind let go, like a rubber band being released, and he became light-headed, but happy. He hadn't realized how scared he'd been to remember. Why had he ever worried? A weight lifted from his chest. "He told me he was proud of me."

"What else?"

"He said I was chosen. That those who had come before me were not worthy, but I was. I had a special knowledge that no one else had."

"How did that make you feel?"

Julian thought for a moment. "Justified. I'd always believed I was special. That was when I knew it was true. That's where it all began. How could I have forgotten about that?"

"Selfish pride. A terrible sin. There is only one who can truly rule, and he needs those he can trust to stand by his side. Harold is already with him, and you can have your place as well if you will stop serving yourself. You have nothing to lose and everything to gain. Asmodeus is a spirit. He needs those of the flesh who can rule in his stead. Use his gifts and wisdom. You rely on your humanity, but there is so much more he can give you."

Julian's blood warmed with a lust for more. He could be more than a king to rule the earth. He could be a god. "And he'll help me accomplish the goals I've set out to complete?"

"You forget they are his goals. What you want is what he wants. Without him you will fail. It is only by his power that you've come this far. The enemy you fight against has power in the spiritual realm. You can't defeat them without your own."

"Is that true?"

"Yes."

"So Tyler was right about the voodoo?"

"Not about that name, but yes."

"And I don't need to drink blood?"

Bea chuckled. "No. I promise."

"Then what do I do?"

"Do you remember the verses we repeated in the mirror?"

"I do now."

"Good. You committed your life to him once. Simply go back and do it again."

"And he'll let me know what is required?"

"He will."

"And what about Katy? Have you been through all of that with her?"

"Not yet. There's no need to rush."

"I thought you said the time was short."

"Your time."

"What?"

"Don't worry. It's not that short. But we can be patient with her. He was something special in mind for her. She will stand on your shoulders, Julian. You can feel proud."

His chest swelled. "I do."

Felix stood against the wall. As an angel, he had seen the whole thing. Julian's dream—the one he couldn't remember—was no dream.

"You don't know what you've done." Felix shook his head sadly. He'd seen it too many times before.

Julian, who had manipulated so many others, did not notice when he himself was being manipulated. His thirst for power blinded him to the truth of what he was giving himself over to.

Julian had done a lot of truly horrifying things in his lifetime, but he couldn't compare to his ancestor. That could all change now.

But one thing was for sure. The man Julian had seen at the foot of his bed as a boy was not his great-great-grandfather. Harold had given himself fully over to the enemy before he died, but when his life finally ended, he was lost forever. There had been no coming back.

Felix had been there to witness Harold's power as it grew.

He'd fought the horde that protected Harold and they'd been able to stop the worst of what the enemy had tried to accomplish. But they all knew it was only a matter of time before they had the same war on their hands.

Guarding Eva as a child had been the easy part. The enemy wasn't aware until it was too late that her Father had called her. Her mind had been protected from the worst of it, but that didn't mean she didn't carry a heavy burden from her past. And it would only get harder.

He waited until Julian and Bea had left the room before passing through the walls, where he walked across the lawn. Dark shadows shrank back from the light that came from him. He knew them and they knew him. They had been there since Harold's time and caused a lot of trouble for Felix when Ben and Eva escaped from this place. It had been a hard-fought battle, but worth it.

Now, he gave them little attention. He was needed elsewhere. Events had been set in motion. Julian's choice to respond to a dark call changed things. They'd all have to be vigilant, especially the humans who forgot too easily that they must trust in their Father without ceasing. He was the only one who would keep them safe and lead them. He was the only one who could rescue them from temptation. They needed Him, but too often, they forgot.

Chapter 7

BEN SET a mug of coffee near Eva, whose head was resting on the table. Neither one of them had slept well that night and they'd left Clara to her snoring, sneaking upstairs to start again on trying to find Lynn.

They'd taken the time to pray for God's help while the coffee was brewing. It was awkward at first. Eva was still unsure where she stood with God, but she conceded to herself that she needed whatever help she could get. On her own, she struggled to keep her head above water.

"You don't have to start this early in the morning, you know," Ben said as he sat down with her at the table. "People will be sleeping."

"I know, but this is too important and if I get the number right, I want to get her before she goes to work." She had been prepared to try the phone after their training session the previous afternoon, but Ben made her wait until today. It had been the right thing to do. Instead of staring at the phone, she'd helped Clara gather supplies from the woods. It was the first time she'd felt like she had a functional part to offer.

Now she held the phone in her hand, attempting to resist the stress that tied her stomach in knots. "I'll find her or I won't. All I can do is try."

"That's right."

She lifted her eyes from the phone to look at him. "Would you mind not sitting here? It makes me nervous."

He pushed back from the table, then opened the door and leaned on the frame, looking out into the lifting gloom as the sun threatened to expose itself to their solitary place in the forest.

She watched the muscles in his back shift as he lifted his mug to take a sip of coffee. When she realized she was staring, she quickly refocused on the phone.

Her cheeks puffed out as she held a puff of air in her mouth, preparing to dial her first number. But she didn't give herself time to think, she just dialed and set the phone to speaker. When it rang, she laid it on the table with her finger poised over the hang-up button.

"It's early," came a woman's voice, coarse with sleep. "And it's my day off. If you're trying to sell me insurance, I will hunt you down and beat you over the head with your phone."

"Uh...Lynn?"

"Depends on who's asking."

Ben spun around.

Eva looked up at him as she spoke. "This—this is Eva." The line was silent. "Lynn?"

"If I ascend to heaven, you are there." Lynn's voice shook.

"If I make my bed in Sheol, you are there," Eva recited. "Is that a code?"

"Is it really you? How did you—I thought—I didn't know what to think. I saw on the news that you were back with Julian."

"I was. I lost my memory. All of it. I didn't know."

"That's what they said, that you had an injury involving your memory. They said you were kidnapped for a ransom, but I thought that was Julian. I didn't know what to believe. I was so afraid Julian had you and it was impossible to get to you. We talked about trying to get you back, but—wait, you said you have no memory at all? Still?"

"Yeah. I've got nothing. I got hit on the head and fell into the river. I remember how to do things, but I have no memory of anyone I've known or anything that I've done." The line was silent again. "Lynn?"

"If you have no memory, how did you call this number and how did you know the verse?"

"I know this doesn't make sense, but I promise you, this isn't some sort of trap. I had this random memory of you. I don't even know who you are."

"Then how'd you get this number?"

"I let my fingers dial—I know it sounds weird and crazy. I don't really understand it myself."

"And the verse?"

"I found it in a drawer in my apartment. I looked up the verse on the internet. That's the only reason I know it."

"So besides random stuff, you have no memory?"

"No. None."

"You don't know who I am?"

"No idea. This call is a risk for both of us. Are we a part of some kind of group? Are we trying to stop Julian?" Lynn didn't respond. "Please." Eva squeezed her eyes closed. "Have I messed up?"

"No. Sorry. This is a lot. I'm just—I need to get some wisdom on this."

"Wisdom?"

"I'm sorry I can't take your word for it, Eva. I want to trust you, but there is too much at stake. I've been praying for this, but I can't assume this is God. Can you call me back in a day or two—no wait, that's too long. If this is real, I need to get to you. Call me in an hour. I'll have a decision by then."

"A decision about what?"

"Whether or not to trust you."

The phone went dead. Eva set it on the table. "I don't understand what just happened."

"Can't say I blame her," Clara said, entering the room. She grabbed a basket off the floor. "I know what's going on and even I think it's hokey. Eggs?"

"Do we have a choice?" Ben said.

"I'll be back."

Eva spun the phone around on the table. "What do we do now?"

"We give her an hour."

"What's going to change in an hour?"

"Time to pray."

"You think she's praying?"

"Sounds to me like she's a Christian. You guys have that scripture as a way of communicating, and she said she's been praying for you. I'd say she's going to spend the next hour asking God for wisdom."

"You don't think that's odd?"

"It's smart. There's no way for her to know if you're setting a trap for her. God's the only one who can communicate that to her."

Eva sagged in her chair. "You think she can trust God with this? What if he doesn't answer her? Or what if she hears him wrong? Or what if there is no God?"

"I know you can't remember, but we have every reason to believe that you trusted in him once. God got you away from Julian twice now."

"I know."

It was a quiet hour while they waited. Eva watched Ben pace around the room while Clara cooked breakfast. "You're sure I can't help you with anything?" Eva asked Clara.

"Nope. This is my happy place. Let me be in my happy place."

Ben finally settled against the doorframe. It seemed to be his favorite spot.

His eyes focused on the floor while his lips moved silently.

"I know what this needs," Clara said, wiping her hands on her apron. "A little bit of parsley."

When she left for the garden, Ben sat down at the table.

"Have you been praying?" Eva asked.

"Yeah."

"But isn't Lynn praying? Why do you need to pray?"

"Prayer is never wasted. I've been asking God to help Lynn hear him clearly."

"Oh. That's smart."

"There's something else. She's not the only one who needs wisdom. We're taking a gamble as well. You can't remember who she is, and there's no way for us to be certain she's on our side."

"But we have no choice."

"There is always a choice. If God says no, then I say no. I hope that's not the case, but if she's not the right person to trust, then we have to believe that God has another way."

"So you've been praying for wisdom too."

"Yeah."

"But I know her number. And she knew that verse. And she's praying. And you're the one who insisted we do this."

"Yes. I know. It all appears to be good, but I want to make sure. We can't rush any of this. I know it feels like we are in a hurry, but we still have to be cautious."

Eva looked at the clock on the wall. "It's been an hour."

"Then call her back."

"So you feel like Lynn is safe?"

"I don't feel anything in my spirit to suggest otherwise."

"What does that mean?"

"What?"

"You feel things in your spirit? How does that work?"

"It's hard to explain. Um. You remember when you cut me free at Julian's?"

"Yes."

"Why did you do it?"

"I just knew it was what I had to do."

"You could feel it."

"I guess."

"It's a similar sort of thing. If I felt no peace about contacting Lynn, I wouldn't let you call her back."

"Oh." Eva stared at the phone, trying to feel a place deep inside of her. But she hadn't been trying when she freed Ben. The understanding was just there. "I don't feel anything."

"That's okay. "

She thought of Lynn, and even though she had no idea if God would speak to her about it, she asked him anyway. *This is your last chance to stop us. If this isn't what you want, you need to tell me now.*

She waited, but with nothing discernible to guide her, she picked up the phone and dialed.

"Eva."

"I'm glad you answered."

"I wish I had more to go on here, but I'm going to trust you."

"That's what God said?"

"As best as I can tell."

Eva looked up at Ben. "I wish he was a little clearer in his direction."

"It's fine. It's enough. So where are you? No, wait. Don't answer that. I can't be sure my phone is secure. Are you safe?"

"Yes."

"Are you alone?"

"No. There are two others here."

"And you're sure you can trust them?"

"Yes. They're the only reason I'm still alive."

"Man. I can't believe this. I really thought we'd lost you. I had moments when I doubted. When I was afraid we were going to lose this war."

"War?"

"Yeah. You're the one who called it that. We're at war and you were one of our generals—so to speak."

"There are others with you?"

"Yeah."

"If we're at war, does that mean we have an army?"

"I wouldn't say that exactly."

"I can't remember any of this," Eva muttered. "Lynn, can you tell us what's going on? We know some small bits, but mostly we have no idea about the bigger picture."

"I can't risk it over the phone. You don't remember the message board where you can leave a message?"

"The cats."

"You do remember?"

"No."

"But you just said—"

"I know." Eva groaned. "Random things keep coming back. I remember the message board about adorable cats, but I don't remember anything else about it."

"So there's no code floating around in that head of yours?"

"Definitely not."

"Then we're going to have to take a risk," Lynn mumbled to herself. "Listen, Eva. Don't tell me exactly where you are, but if you tell me somewhere I can meet you, we can make sure I wasn't followed."

"I'll be able to tell if she was followed," Ben said.

"Who's that?"

"One of the two people on the planet who I trust right now. I hope you'll make it three. I could use more. Okay. Do you know the town where I was rescued?"

"Yeah."

"What are you thinking?" Ben said.

"Roger's store. Will that work?"

"As good as any."

"What's Roger's store?" Lynn said.

"A handyman store in the middle of town on the main street. You can't miss it. If you wait there, out the front, we'll meet you there."

"Okay, let me check how far that is from me…got it. I'll get some things together and meet you there not long after dark."

"See you then." Eva hung up. "You still feel good about this?" she said to Ben.

"I think we can trust her, yeah. What about you?"

"Same. Clara?"

"You want my opinion?"

"It's your house we're bringing her back to," Eva said.

"I'm willing to take the risk if you two are."

Ben looked at his watch. "It's going to be a long day, but when the time comes, Clara, you stay here. Eva and I will pick her up."

"I knew you were going to say that."

"Sorry, but I don't want us all going out at the same time. Just in case. If I don't honk the horn twice as we come down the road, then you get in that bunker and hide. Eva, you and I will park the car somewhere out of town and walk in. We don't want anyone to see Clara's truck and start asking questions."

"I didn't think of that. Maybe I should call her back and suggest somewhere else."

"No, town's good because there are more places to stay out of sight than on a long stretch of road. It will be simple enough. Once we establish she hasn't been followed, you go jump in her car and lead her back to the truck. We just need to keep our heads down. We don't want anyone knowing we're in town either."

Ben kept himself busy for the day by doing repairs on the house while Eva practiced throwing the knife.

The sun was setting when Ben approached her near the shed.

"That post is looking destroyed," Ben said when he sidled up next to her.

"I've only hit the target a couple of times."

"You don't see that as a good thing?"

"No. A few times is not regular."

"Maybe you need a break."

"I had one already."

"Then it's time for another. It's time to go, anyway. We need to be in position before Lynn arrives so we can make sure no one else is watching."

She tossed the knife one last time, and it missed the target by several inches. She stared at it until Ben pulled her away. "Let's go."

They were still a few miles out of town when Ben felt them. He pulled the car over.

"What is it? Did you see something?" Eva asked.

"I don't know. We need to pray."

"Why?" Eva shifted in her seat. She looked out into the darkness.

"It's hard to explain. But I can feel that something's not right." *How could he tell her he felt like demons were closing in on them?*

"Like a warning?"

"Kind of."

"Is it Lynn?"

"I don't think so."

"But you don't know?"

"Do you mind if I pray out loud?"

"Not if that's what you need to do."

Eva closed her eyes and bowed her head. It made Ben smile to see her respond in that way. If she never remembered God from her life before, he'd make sure he did whatever he could to bring her back to him again.

"God, we need your help here. If we need to turn around and head back, let me know. We'll do it. Don't let us make a mistake."

He waited, fumbling different words through his mind to try to find a sense of what God was trying to say. "Cover us," he finally said. "Don't let them see."

He opened his eyes and looked at Eva, who still had her eyes closed. "Amen."

"Amen." She looked up at him. "What did you mean?"

"About what?"

"What you said at the end. 'Don't let them see.' Don't let who see? Do you think someone has followed Lynn here?"

"No, but the closer I got to town, the more I felt like something was off. I can't really explain it beyond that. I don't think we need to turn around, but I do think we need God near us right now."

"Why?"

"Sometimes I can sense when demons are around."

"Demons?"

"Yeah. And I've seen at least one angel."

"That's crazy."

"Maybe, but you have prophetic dreams."

"Since when?"

"You dreamed about me being tied to the chair."

"That was a fever dream."

"Was it?"

"Well...there have actually been times in my short memory when I've sensed a dark presence coming after me."

"Really?"

"After you rescued me from Clara's, when I was at the hospital, I fell asleep and had this horrible dream that a wolf was after me." She looked out into the dark. "It said, 'Welcome back.'"

"Wow."

"I thought it was a bad dream, but after everything that's happened since then, I'm not so sure."

"No, I don't think that was a dream. At least not in the traditional sense. But either way, the wolf was wrong. You were back, but only for a short time and only because God needed to use you there."

"You really think there are demons out there?" She nodded toward the road ahead.

"I do."

"What do we do?"

"We continue our plan. I'm ready to turn back, but I don't think we need to."

"I sure hope you're right."

Chapter 8

"STOP WALKING SO STIFF," Ben said as he attempted to meander into town. "We need to look like a regular couple out for an evening stroll."

They had dropped the truck off on a dark, dead-end side road with no residences to keep it out of sight.

Eva took a slow, deep breath. "I'm sorry. I'm worried someone will look out their window and recognize one of us. My picture was all over the news and you lived here."

Ben grabbed her hand. "No one will believe it's me walking into town with a girl." He shook her arm when her fingers didn't close around his. "Unless, of course, she looks like she's being forced to hold my hand."

"You're right." Her hand relaxed into his. "But I don't see why it would be weird for the town to see you walking around with a woman. Seems like a normal thing for a man to do."

"This town has never seen me as normal. I may not

have scared them as much as Clara and Franky, but most people in town gave me a wide berth."

"Why?"

"They were waiting for the crazy loner to crack."

"Just because you lived on your own?"

"No. When I first moved into town, there was an incident."

"What kind of incident?"

"I was outside Roger's store when a car backfired. I had a flashback of when I blew up Julian's facility. I lost it. Enough people saw. Roger ran out of his store and calmed me down, but not before he copped one on the chin."

"You punched Roger in the face?"

"Not punched exactly. I was flailing around and he got too close. I nearly knocked him out."

"I guess I'd be wary of you, too, if I saw something like that."

"Yeah."

"Although not as wary as your talk about demons has made me." She looked around at the dark shadows surrounding them.

"You don't seem the type to spook easily."

"I probably didn't used to be."

"Don't worry about it. There's nothing they can do to us, even if they are around."

"Then why did we have to stop and pray?"

"It wasn't because I was worried they'd jump from the bushes with a gun."

"What if one did jump from the bushes?"

"I don't think they do that."

"But what if one did?"

Ben laughed. "I'd probably tell him to get lost."

"That's it? You don't have some holy water or a cross to throw at him?"

"Don't need it. I've got a sword."

Eva's smile stopped at a lopsided grin. "You're serious?"

"The Bible is a sword."

"The Bible."

"Yeah."

"A book."

"Yup."

"I hope I don't get to find out if it would really work or not."

"It does. I've used it before."

"I'll have to take your word for it."

Felix stood with his arms crossed in the alley. The light from his robes filled the space around him, blocking any view of the street at his back.

"What are you doing here?" a dark thing snarled from the only scrap of shadow it could find to cower in.

"If I'm not mistaken, I can go wherever I choose."

The thing's lips curled up in an ugly snort. "Not wherever. You have limitations, just like I do. Someone called you."

"And what if they did?"

"Who was it?"

Felix smiled. "I am not at liberty to divulge that information."

"You wouldn't tell me, anyway."

"No, probably not."

"*I'm* still going to tell."

"Tell what?"

"That you're here. It isn't for no reason."

"That's correct. I rarely turn up somewhere for no reason. Come to think of it, I always have a reason for everywhere I go. But I'm sure your superiors will be overjoyed with the fount of information you will bring to them." He looked over his shoulder as Ben and Eva passed by.

"You're trying to keep me from joining the others, aren't you?"

"I have nothing to say to that."

"Doesn't matter. You can't stay here all night."

"I could," Felix said. "But there's no need and I have other matters to attend to."

The thing jumped up, hopping from one clawed foot to the other in anticipation of freedom. "Then off you go."

Felix pursed his lips as he looked down at the squirming thing. A team of angels had made their presence felt in a nearby town, drawing most of the other demons away. That left Felix to deal with a few stragglers who had been forced to stay. But one thing Felix could always count on was that those left behind would risk the consequences of disobeying orders just to be contrary to an angel.

He offered the cowering thing a quick nod before he vanished.

The demon sprang forward, flying out of the alley. His focus was completely taken up by his new destination, so he didn't notice the newcomers in town.

Ben and Eva continued their casual walk until they turned the corner onto the main street and both stopped dead in their tracks.

"This way," Ben whispered as he pulled Eva across to the other side of the road. They continued a few steps until a building concealed them from the crowd of people that were hovering outside the pizza place across the street from Roger's shop.

"I forgot about Pizza Plaza," Ben said, taking another look down the road.

"Not a fan of pizza?"

"It's new. The grand opening."

"What's the problem?"

"The people. Normally, the street is quiet."

"But we can use this. With so many people around, no one is going to notice us."

"We can't risk it. From far away, no one might recognize either one of us, but if we get too close, we can't be sure they won't."

Another group of people walked down the road, passing the street Ben and Eva were on. He flattened her against the wall, covering her body with his until they'd passed. A minute later, the group erupted in an off-key "Happy Birthday" song.

Ben checked around the corner again. "They're filling the street."

"What do we do?"

"Call Lynn. We'll sort out another rendezvous." Ben waited for Eva to make the call, but she just looked at him. "Aren't you going to call?"

"Don't you have the phone?"

He closed his eyes. "No."

"I guess we'll have to figure something else out. Do you think you could pray them away?"

"Seriously?"

Eva shrugged. "Just trying to think outside the box."

"Anything is worth a shot. Would you like to do the honors?"

Her eyes widened. "Me?"

"Why not?"

"I'm not a Christian."

"I'm pretty sure you are."

"I don't think it counts if I can't remember."

He wanted to argue with her, but had no idea what he would even say. "Okay." He closed his eyes. "God, can you move the people out of the way? Or do you have a better idea?"

They waited, and the party on the street continued with no hint of letting up.

"Is that a no?" Eva said. "Does that mean God has a better idea?"

"He must, 'cause I got an idea. Keep your head

down and follow me." He headed down the side street and around the block.

"Where are we going?"

"I'm going to break into Roger's store."

"That doesn't sound like a better idea."

"It'll work. You told Lynn to wait outside the hardware store. When she arrives, I'll get her attention from inside the store and tell her to meet us back down the road. That way no one can make a connection between her and us."

"What if you set off Roger's security?"

"He doesn't have any."

"You're sure?"

"Sure enough."

"What if Lynn doesn't get out of her car?"

"She will."

"How do you know?"

"Because she has to."

"Okay. What about me? What do you want me to do?"

"I want you to have eyes on the front. Find a good vantage point and make sure there's no one watching or following."

"Okay, I can do that. Then do you want me to meet you at Olive Lane?"

"How'd you know it was Olive Lane?"

"Because that's where the little alleyway goes out at Roger's back door."

"And how'd you know that?"

"I've been in his store, remember?"

"The first time we met." The corner of his mouth curled up slightly when he remembered their first encounter. It was the last thing he would have expected that day.

"Yeah. I was frustrated at myself for looking for an escape route when I didn't need one."

"Frustrated?"

"Have you forgotten that I'm afraid of the person I used to be?"

"I haven't forgotten, but I hoped you were less afraid of her now."

Eva studied the streetlight. Bugs darted through the beam. "I honestly don't know. The idea of a normal life is enticing, but in the small bursts that I get a taste of it, it doesn't fit right."

"I know the feeling. Maybe it's because we haven't had a chance to embrace it. Deep down, we've both been waiting for something bad to happen."

"Now that it has, I guess it's more useful to embrace who we really are."

They both were still for a moment, looking at each other, unsure what to say or do next.

Eva broke the silence. "You better go. She could be here soon and I need to get back out the front."

Ben nodded. "See you on the other side." He jogged down the road and around to the back of Roger's shop. After he disappeared, Eva looked around her. It was dark and there were too many shadows hiding the unknown, so she hurried back to a place they were before and watched for Lynn's arrival.

Ben kept his face pointed to the ground as he turned down the alley. The shadows pressed close, and he prayed under his breath as he pulled the tools he needed from his pocket. He didn't even know why he'd brought them in the first place. But God obviously did.

He listened as a car drove by not too far away, then he crouched down and set to work on the lock.

It had been a while since he'd had to do anything like this, and he felt a small amount of triumph when the lock turned.

Inside, he hurried to the front of the store, keeping himself hidden behind the shelves while he got into a position where he could see outside.

Part of the crowd had moved back closer to the pizza place, but the black sedan that arrived soon after still had to park in front of the shop next door.

"Please get out. Please get out." He focused on the car, praying the plan would work.

After a couple of tense moments, a woman in her forties wearing an off-white silk blouse and a pencil skirt got out of the car. She looked at the crowd, then pulled out her phone and walked casually toward the store, engrossed by her screen. When she reached the store, she looked around, then stood close to the front door.

She had no urgency in her manner to arouse suspicion, and she had placed herself close enough to the group that she looked like she was an uninterested part of it.

Ben skirted around a display of tools to the front

door. She was close enough that he would only have to open the door a crack to be able to speak to her without drawing attention to either of them. It was going to work.

He reached for the lock when a gun cocked behind him.

Chapter 9

AFTER THE SOUND of the gun, several thoughts fought for Ben's attention. The first was an attempt to figure out how Julian had found them, but it didn't matter. The man had eyes and ears everywhere. They all knew meeting with Lynn was risky, and they had all decided it was a risk worth taking. But his own safety was not what was causing him the most grief in this moment. If Julian had found *him*, then he may have found Eva too. Or if not, it was impossible for him to warn her. He quickly pushed the thought aside and focused on his present problem.

After a quick prayer to heaven, he lifted his hands in surrender while noting the wrenches hanging nearby. They were within reach.

As he turned, his muscles tensed and his hand was ready to pluck the tool from the shelf and fling it at his foe.

"Ben?"

At the sound of his assailant's voice, Ben's shoulders

sagged and his fingers retreated into a loose fist as he turned, keeping his hands up. "Roger. Hi."

"What are you doing here? I thought you were one of those kids from outside getting into trouble."

"I…uh. How'd you even know I was in here? It's well past closing."

"I got this new security system with an app thingy. It alerts me if anything's moving in the store once I've closed up."

"Oh. Good idea. Listen, I, uh, I needed some more things for the fence I'm building."

"It couldn't wait until morning?" The frown on Roger's face was skeptical.

"I was going to pay."

"Ben, I know you've got your troubles, but looting my store? I didn't think you were the type. Are you short on money? 'Cause if you are, all you need to do is ask for help. You know I'll do what I can to help you out."

"No, I'm not here to steal from you. I'm really sorry. I just…" He cringed. He still needed to talk to Lynn. He knew of a way that Roger might let him finish the job, but he didn't like it. "The truth is, I needed a place to hide."

"Hide? From who? Those guys out there? You know they're harmless, right? Just some kids celebrating a birthday. I know I said I thought one of them had broken in, but they're not here to harm you."

Ben sucked on his teeth. He knew he could play on Roger's perception of him. He needed to get the store owner to dismiss Ben as a delusional man and indulge him for only a few minutes.

"Not them," Ben said, preparing for what he was about to say. "There are people after me."

"What people?"

"From the government. They've been watching me for months."

Roger's face fell and all Ben could do was offer him a painful smile. "Is this because of that incident with the FBI coming into town?" Roger said.

"Yes, exactly."

"Ben"—Roger set the gun aside, making sure it was out of Ben's reach—"they were here to save that poor woman. Do you remember her? You ran into her when you were in my store the last time. The Palmers kidnapped her. The FBI wasn't here for you. They were here for her."

"That was their cover."

"Listen, I know a place you can be safe."

"You do?"

"Yes. Why don't you let me take you to the hospital? They'll have someone you can talk to about all of this. I promise you'll be safe there."

Ben fidgeted with the hem of his shirt. "Not yet. Please, Roger. You've got to believe me. I need five more minutes and they'll move out and then I can leave here."

Roger's lips puckered to the side. His pity was obvious. "I'll tell you what. I'll give you five more minutes if you promise to come with me to the hospital afterward."

"You'll let me stay?"

"For five minutes."

"Okay. Deal."

Roger picked up his gun again, but didn't move. Ben sighed. "You can't wait here."

"Why not?"

"Because they'll see you."

Roger sidestepped out of view from the window. "Is this better?"

"I'd prefer if you waited out the back. That way, I know you're safe."

"I'd prefer to keep an eye on you."

"You don't trust me. I guess I can't blame you."

"It's not that." Roger shifted his weight onto his back foot. "Okay. I'll wait out the back if that makes you more comfortable."

"It would. Thank you."

Roger hesitated, but then headed toward the back door. Ben waited until he was out of sight before rushing to the front door. Lynn was still there, waiting.

He monitored the surrounding people, then opened the door a crack.

"Lynn, don't turn around. Don't acknowledge that you're talking to me. I'm Ben. Eva's watching you from down the road. She's watching from a distance to make sure you weren't followed, but with all these people here, we can't risk being seen. I need you to get back in your car and continue down this road. Take your third right and drive about two miles. There is a sign there showing how far it is to the highway. Pull over at the sign. Eva and I will meet you there."

Lynn didn't react except to tuck her phone back into her purse before walking back to her car.

Ben relocked the front door, then exited out the back, where he found Roger waiting as promised.

"Coast is clear?" he asked.

"Uh, yeah. About that." Ben shook his head. "I'm sorry you had to see that. I feel like an idiot. I'm actually okay."

"You're not going to get out of it that easy. You promised me you'd go."

"I know. And a few minutes ago I needed to. You were right. But I'm better now."

"Ben…"

"I've snapped out of it. I was triggered earlier today."

"What happened?"

"I had a terrible dream. A, uh…a flashback. I remember the FBI turning up to save that woman. I know that's why they were here. But when I woke up from that dream, I—I don't know—I guess my brain was a bit scrambled and I was confused. If you hadn't come in when you did, I'd probably still be confused, but you snapped me out of it. I realize now how ridiculous I'm being. No one's watching me, and I'm sorry for upsetting you."

Roger nodded sharply. "I'm not upset, but I am glad to hear your mind is clear. And I'm glad I could help. But I'd still like to take you to the hospital and let them check you over and make sure you're okay."

"I don't want to waste their time. Not now when I'm feeling better." Roger sighed and Ben could see he still wasn't convinced. "I've got an appointment," he continued. "With my shrink. Tomorrow. I'll talk to him about it then. He'll know what to do." He hated lying to Roger like this.

"I didn't realize you were seeing anyone."

"Just started. I know I need help and he's been great."

"You think you'll be okay for tonight? What if you have another bad dream?"

"I've got pills I can take."

"What kind of pills?"

"Don't worry, they're prescription. They're to help me sleep. I don't like to take them, but I will tonight. I won't have any more dreams tonight."

"Okay. Good. You want me to give you a lift home?"

"No. My truck's not far. Listen, I really appreciate you looking out for me. More than you could know."

Roger patted Ben on the arm. "Anytime. Just make me one more promise?"

"What's that?"

"Go straight home. Don't stop anywhere. And if you start feeling like someone's out to get you, you call me, got it? I'll come to you no matter where you are."

Ben couldn't speak for a moment. He had no idea to what lengths Roger had been prepared to go for him. "You're a good man, Roger. Thank you. You've been a good friend to me."

"No need to thank me. I'm not doing anything special. I just don't like to think of you on your own. It's not good for a man to be alone. "

"It's more uncommon than you realize. You've got a good heart and you shouldn't minimize that. There aren't a lot who would go out of their way like you're prepared to do. Never lose that. But you don't have to worry about me. I'll be okay."

"I hope so." He turned to lock the door and Ben made his way out of the alley before Eva had time to turn up. He didn't want to risk Roger seeing her. They didn't have time to answer more questions.

Lynn sat in her car waiting when Ben pulled up behind her.

When Eva didn't make a move to get out, Ben said, "Do you want me to go?"

"No. She knows me. I should go." She put her hand on the door handle but hesitated. "I don't know why I'm nervous about seeing her. I won't know her just like everyone else."

"But she was a friend."

"As far as we know."

"I can go if you want."

Eva opened the door. "No. I'll do it."

She moved stiffly toward Lynn's car and a woman she didn't recognize got out.

Eva scanned her hands to check for a weapon but saw fists with white knuckles. She looked over the rest of Lynn now that they were closer. Her dark hair shone in the headlights and her skin was pale, but Eva couldn't be sure if it was that color naturally or if Lynn was afraid.

"When it took you so long to get here," Lynn said while Eva was still a few feet away, "I was worried something had happened."

"Sorry about that. We had to park the truck outside of town. We didn't want to risk it being seen. People would know Clara's vehicle around town."

"Clara?"

"Another friend."

"Right. I'm glad you found people to keep you safe. I guess we should be thanking God for that."

Eva frowned. "Yeah."

"Did I say something wrong?"

"No. It's just that God is the same as everyone else. I can't remember him."

"Oh. That makes sense. So you don't remember God and I take it I don't look familiar to you at all?"

"No, I'm sorry."

"You don't have to apologize."

"I thought I was hoping you would be familiar, but it turns out I'm relieved I don't know you." The words Eva spoke were true, but she didn't know why she said them out loud.

"Why does that make you relieved?"

"I don't know."

"Then I guess I'm glad one of us is relieved. I did have hope that my presence would trigger your memory, because without that, we are in big trouble."

"But that's why we tried to contact you. If you're working on this, too, don't you know what we were doing?"

"We can't overlook the miracle that you're still alive and you're safe from Julian, but it's still a big setback."

Eva nodded. A knot formed in her stomach. She looked up and down the road. "We should get going. It didn't look like anyone was following you, but we need to be safe."

"Then why didn't we meet out here in the first place? Town was crowded."

"That was unexpected. But we couldn't meet here. It's a straight road for miles. If anyone had been following you, we wouldn't have gotten away. In town, there are more places to hide."

"Right. That is a whole other world of thinking from where I come from."

"Is it?"

"Yeah."

"I was hoping we were similar."

Lynn laughed, but then stifled it. "We couldn't be more different from any other two people."

"We'll have to worry about that later. You can follow us back."

"Back where?"

"We're staying with a friend. It's a property about an hour from here."

Lynn looked back at the truck where Ben was waiting behind the wheel. "That's Ben?"

"Yeah."

"You're certain he's not working for Julian?"

"I'm more certain about trusting him than I am about trusting you."

"Then let's get out of here."

Chapter 10

BEN KEPT his eyes on the long driveway, but his attention was focused on his peripheral where the shadows took over outside the headlights. He didn't sense any danger and honked twice before the house was in sight.

Clara waited for them on the porch, braced against the post with her rifle nestled into her shoulder. It was aimed unwaveringly at Lynn's car as it parked.

Eva jumped out of the truck. "It's safe, Clara. You can put the gun down. Didn't you hear the double honk?"

"You can guarantee she's not one of them?"

"She has to trust us as much as we have to trust her," Ben said, as he positioned himself between Lynn and Clara.

"I don't reckon I agree." Clara scrunched up her mouth. "I think she's got the upper hand here. But don't worry. I won't shoot 'er if I don't hafta."

Lynn got out of her car slowly, with her hands raised, but she remained behind the car door.

"Clara," Ben said. "Put the gun away or I'll come over there and take it from you."

Clara huffed, but finally pointed the weapon at the ground. "I'll warn you I'm a quick draw."

"I'm sure you are. Lynn, I'd like you to meet Clara. She's very cautious."

"As long as you're sure she won't shoot me, I don't mind. I'm no good at dodging bullets. Administration, on the other hand, I can do."

Clara kept the gun gripped tightly in her hands as Eva led Lynn into the house, but she rested it against the wall once they were all inside.

"So, how do you guys all know each other?" Lynn asked when Eva invited her to sit at the table.

"Clara was the one who rescued me from the river."

Lynn's eyes darted to Clara, then quickly dropped to the table before looking back at Eva. "Isn't she…"

"Isn't she what?" Clara sat heavy in the chair next to Lynn and leaned toward her.

"Nothing. I just thought…nothing."

"Yes," Eva said. "This is the place the FBI found me. But I can assure you everything is fine. I trust Clara with my life and Ben too. It's a long story I'd rather not rehash at the moment."

"That's fine. We've all decided to trust one another, so we're going with that."

"You two decided to trust her." Clara snorted. "I didn't have much of a say in it."

"You didn't protest when we left to meet with her," Ben said.

"You've been gone awhile and I've had time to think about it."

Eva sighed. "And what are your bones telling you right now? Are they saying Lynn isn't trustworthy?"

Clara's face dropped into the frown that made her look like a frog. "Fine." She got up from the table, grabbed her gun, and headed down the hall toward her room. "I'm going to go give this a clean, if you'll excuse me."

"She'll warm up," Eva said.

Ben joined them at the table. "Clara is never warm. But you get used to it."

"Don't listen to him. Now, Lynn, I don't mean to rush things. But with my memory loss, we're in the dark here. Can you take us through what you know? What is my connection to you? What have I been working on?"

Lynn picked at her fingernail. "I wish I could."

"What?" Ben said.

"I wish I knew everything that was going on, but, Eva, you were very careful."

"I didn't trust you?"

"It wasn't that. You wanted to protect me—all of us —so you only told me what I needed to know. All I can tell you is my part. Like I told you before, I'm not experienced in the stuff you are. I work in the White House. I don't shoot guns. I don't do this dangerous stuff."

"But you are in danger."

"Yeah, but only because I'm involved. The stuff you did was way beyond me."

"Anything you can tell us is more than we've got right now," Ben said. "Why don't you tell us what your part was?"

"My job has been to keep my ear to the ground at the White House. Supply information where I could. Keep track of any influence Julian had."

"Why the White House?"

"Julian is planning something big. That's one thing I do know. There's a bill related to privacy that he is trying to get passed, but I don't know what he's going to do with it. All we've been doing is keeping our ears open and waiting for you, Eva."

"We. You said there was more."

"Not many. And none of us knows how to fight, but we have influence where you need it."

"Influence?"

Lynn's eyes shifted. "We're all based in Washington, DC. I called them after you did."

"And?"

"And they're praying. But they don't want to be identified until I can be sure you can be trusted."

"Do any of them know more about what's going on?" Ben said. "We need their knowledge."

"They know as much as I do. Eva was the mastermind."

"Okay," Eva said. "One step at a time, remember? Can you give us more detail on the bill that Julian is trying to get passed?"

"It gives full power to the president to do basically whatever he wants in the event of an imminent catastrophic terrorist event."

"You mean," Clara said, appearing in the doorway, "they'll keep doing what they're already doing, they just won't need to hide it?"

Lynn looked silently at Eva.

Eva gave her an intimate shake of the head to dismiss Clara's comments. "From what I understand of Julian, the bill sounds like it's up his alley, but I can see the appeal to the general public. We must be talking about the destruction of the country, not just one bombing. What's the definition of a catastrophic terrorist event? Would it be like another 9/11?"

"It would have to be more than that. But what you have to understand is that this bill is about complete control and access."

"Even if that's true, Julian is not the president, so how would this help him?"

"I don't know. You never told me that."

"But I did know?"

"I assume you did. You knew a lot you didn't share."

"With anyone?"

"No."

"I shouldn't be surprised. I already know I wasn't a very good person."

"You shared with me some of your past, but that person you were is not who you are. The only thing you were worried about was the extra danger we would be in if we knew too much. You carried a great deal of the responsibility and cared for each of us deeply. If I would criticize you for anything, it would be that you carried too much of the burden on your own."

"Well, you were right because my caution is working

against us now." Eva leaned back in the chair and ran her fingers through her hair. "Maybe Julian has a way to get access to the information if the president has it. Does he have access to the president?"

"Not as far as I know. Not directly."

"But it doesn't matter, does it?" Ben said. "Even in the event you described, once the threat was gone, if Julian had access, he would soon lose it whether he had the president in his pocket or not. There has to be more."

"If there is, it's locked away in Eva's head. Even the list is no good to us."

"What list?"

"Eva, you had a list of people in the House and Senate who Julian had influence over. People you believe would be voting for the bill. You were going to send it to me so we could work on changing the minds of those who we could."

"That's great. We don't need to understand what Julian is going to do. We already know that we were attempting to stop the bill, so we can still do that without fully understanding why. Where's the list now?"

"That's why I said it wouldn't help. We can't get to it."

"Why not?"

"You kept it hidden in your desk at work."

Eva's head dropped. "So we're still no better off than we were before. Why didn't I send it to you already?"

"You were going to deliver it to me personally because we couldn't risk sending it digitally."

"I guess I ran out of time. Did I give you any of the names? Were you expected to look into all of them?"

"Most of them. With the people I work with. But you said you'd look into one or two personally."

"Who?" Ben said.

"I have no idea."

Eva sighed. "So without that list, we don't even have a place to start."

"Could we talk to everyone who's voting?" Ben asked.

"We don't have time."

Eva rested her head in her hand. "This is impossible. Every time we think we get a break, we lose it."

"Could we break in to Eva's old office?" Clara chimed in.

"We don't have the equipment," Ben said. "Or the time."

Eva's back straightened. "Wait. We don't need to break in. I can walk in and get it."

"You're joking, right?" Lynn said.

"No. This could work. When I was staying with Julian, I met my old boss."

"What difference does that make? Surely he knows by now that you helped me escape," Ben said.

"Maybe he does, but it doesn't matter."

"How can you say that? If you show your face to him, he'll give you to Julian. There's no way you're doing this. We'll have to find another way. This won't work."

"Before you dismiss our one option, at least hear me out."

"Fine." Ben crossed his arms. "But I don't see how any explanation will change anything."

"When I met Michael at Julian's house, he said—" She pressed her lips together. She hadn't properly thought out what she would need to say to explain herself. It was too late to turn back now. "He said we'd been in a relationship before I lost my memory."

"Oh." Ben looked startled. "Hang on, Michael? You mean the Michael who charmed you into relaxation? You never said he was your boss or that you were in a relationship with him."

"I have no idea if I was or not. I can't remember. My point is, while he was there, he made it clear that he was still interested."

"And you made it clear that you were as well?"

Eva sighed, ignoring the flush in her cheeks. They needed to be confident she could pull this off. She'd have to ignore her embarrassment. "Yes."

"You're sure?"

"Yes. Very. I *was* interested."

"Oh my," Clara said with a smirk.

"Give me a break. I was scared and lost. I was looking for any kind of life raft I could get my hands on."

"So you got your hands on him as well?" Clara mumbled.

"Now you're just being cruel. He's a good-looking guy who knew all the right things to say, and I was confused. It obviously wouldn't have worked in the end."

"You sure about that?" Ben said.

"Yes, now we can drop it. The only thing that matters right now is that he doesn't see me as a threat."

Ben frowned. "No, I guess he doesn't."

"And I can use that. I'll call him and tell him I want to meet him at the office."

"What if he tells Julian?"

"I'll ask him not to."

"And you think that will work?"

"I don't know. But I think so. He's the type of guy who's confident of his own ability. I don't think he'll want Julian there to interfere. Not at first, anyway."

"I still don't think this is a good idea," Lynn said. "There has to be a better way. We can't risk you."

"You're going to have to. I'm no use to you right now any other way without my memory and this is all we have. There's no other way and we can't move forward without that list."

"She's right," Ben said. "I don't like it, but it's the best we've got and we're running out of time."

Eva had nearly pulled her hair out when Ben insisted they take time to pray. They had already agreed it was their only move, and she was tired of waiting. But finally, she made the call to Michael's office. The others stood nearby, listening.

"Can I speak to Michael Rosenbloom, please?" Eva said when the receptionist answered.

"Can I tell him who's calling?"

"Yes, it's Eva and can you tell him it's urgent?"

She was only on hold for several seconds before the phone clicked.

"Eva? Is that really you?"

"Hi, yes. Thank you for taking my call."

"I'm surprised to hear from you. Is everything okay?"

"You don't have to pretend, Michael. I'm sure Julian has told you what happened? You must already know how big of a mess I made."

"Yes. Julian told me."

"I never meant for it to happen, I swear. I didn't know what I was doing. One minute I was helping my dad and the next I was knocking Tyler out. I don't even know how I did it. I messed up so bad."

"Eva, calm down. I'm sure we can work this out. Take a breath."

"I knew I could call you. I knew you'd believe me. I have no one else to turn to." She forced tears into her eyes, letting the pain from the past weeks spill out. She already knew Michael wanted her. He'd made that clear. He wouldn't be able to resist coming to her rescue. "You said we were together before I lost my memory. I was hoping you still cared about me enough to help me."

"Eva, of course I'll help you. I'll do anything for you. Where are you?"

"I'm nowhere. I've been wandering around, terrified."

"You should have called me sooner."

"I know. I would have. I've been so scared. I messed up really bad."

"Tell me where you are. I'll come to you."

SHAWNA COLEING

"No. I'd rather come to you."

"I'm at the office. Do you know where that is? Can you get here?"

"Yeah. Dad told me about it. What time do you close? I'll come then. I don't want to risk seeing anyone."

"Are you sure? I think you should come now."

"No. I can't. Please. Will you meet me there after closing?"

"Everyone should be out of the office by seven. I'll wait for you."

"Can you promise me something?"

"Whatever you need."

"Please don't tell my dad. I feel so bad. Please, swear to me you won't tell him. I just need you." Her nose scrunched as the words came from her mouth. It was what he wanted to hear, but it made her sick to say it.

"I won't tell him. I promise. And, Eva?"

"Yeah?"

"You did the right thing calling me."

"I know. I knew deep down that you'd be there for me."

"I'll see you soon."

Eva hung up and dried her tears before looking up at the others.

Clara lifted her hands and did a slow clap. "That was quite a performance."

Judging by the frown on Ben's face, Clara must have been stating a fact that he wasn't sure he agreed with. Eva was compelled to make her place clear. "It made me

106

sick to do it. I know I got taken in by him before, but with what I know now about Julian, it's horrible."

Lynn shook her head. "Well, Clara's right. You did great. He'll have no idea how disgusted you are by the thought of him. Are you sure you're up for this?"

"It doesn't make any difference. Did I ever tell you where I kept the list in my office?"

"You said you had a secret compartment in one of your drawers."

"Which office was mine? I guess I could ask Michael."

"As you leave the elevator and head down the hall on the left, it's the second door on the left. Michael's office is at the end of that hall."

"Great. Wish me luck."

Chapter 11

IT WAS a quiet ride into the city that night. Ben pulled the truck onto the side of the road a few blocks from the office. Lynn put a hand on Eva's arm before she could get out of the car.

"We'll be praying."

"Be careful," Ben added as she opened the door.

Eva gave them each a tight nod before getting out of the car.

"She'll be okay," Lynn said to Ben as they watched Eva cross the road.

"Was that a question or a statement?"

"I'm not sure."

"We prayed about it and we were confident to move forward. That's what we have to focus on."

"Do you ever have doubts? When God sends you to do something dangerous? Do you ever question if you heard him right?"

Lynn's question tickled the sick feeling in Ben's stomach. "I couldn't afford to doubt. But there have been times when I thought I was sure, and it turned out I was too caught up in my own needs—there he is." They saw a man at the door letting Eva in. "I guess that's him."

"Yeah, that's Michael."

"You met him while you were working there?"

"Only briefly."

"You don't look impressed."

"Eva said that Michael told her they used to date, but that's not the impression I got."

"Why didn't you say something?"

"Because I don't know for sure. Eva never mentioned it, but she wasn't friendly with him at the time."

"Maybe they had broken up."

"Maybe. Either way, he must still like her, and that will work for us."

After Eva disappeared inside, Ben leaned back in the seat. An unease had been building, and when he saw the embrace that Michael gave her, his peace had obliterated. The problem now was to discern whether it was his own ignored feelings for Eva, or was it a warning from above?

"This was our only option," Ben said to himself.

"Was that a question or a statement?" Lynn laughed. It had a nervous waver to it.

"Exactly. We all felt right about coming here, right?"

"Don't you become indecisive. I'm relying on your fortitude to get me through this. You said yourself that we prayed about it and were confident moving forward. Has that changed?"

"I don't feel right about this."

"Ben!" She twisted sharply in her seat. "Why didn't you say something before?"

"Because I believed it was the right thing before."

"Okay, slow down. I'm starting to panic. I can't panic. Let's think about this rationally. We all agreed to do this, and you were all for it until you saw Michael…"

"What is that look for?"

"Do you believe your concern is discernment speaking or something else?"

"You think it's something else?"

Lynn looked back at the building. "Look, Ben, we barely know each other, but I saw the look on your face when she talked about being charmed by Michael. I heard what you said."

"Are you saying I shouldn't be protective?"

"No. We should all be protective of one another. But if your feelings for Eva are clouding your judgment, then I'm the one who needs to be protective."

"There's nothing going on between us."

"Maybe not, but we can't stop the only plan we have because you don't like the idea of Michael hitting on Eva. If that's not what this is, then fine, let's do something about it. But unless you have some sort of plan, she's already inside and there's nothing to be done about it but wait."

Ben grimaced. "I don't know what my feelings are and I don't know what to do."

"Then we better pray until we get some clarity."

"I was afraid you'd say that."

"But I'm right."

"Yes. You are."

Eva had given Michael a beaming smile and endured a tight embrace before being led upstairs.

"You didn't call my dad?" she said as they rode in the elevator.

"I told you I wouldn't. No one knows you're here but me. I'm quite content to have you all to myself. Especially if it's what you want."

"I didn't know who else to turn to."

He slid an arm around her and pulled her close to his side. "You made the right choice. I'll protect you."

"I can't tell you how much that means to me. After everything I've been through and then what I did…I don't know what I would have done if you never forgave me for what I did to my dad."

"We all make mistakes."

"But you're risking your relationship with him for doing this."

"Not really. He trusts me and when this is all cleared up he'll probably give me a raise for looking after you so well."

"Do you really think he could ever forgive me?"

"He cares about you a great deal. I can't promise there won't be consequences—"

"Consequences?"

"You'll have to earn back his trust."

"If I ever can."

"You've got nothing to worry about. I'll look after you every step of the way."

When the doors opened on the seventh floor,

Michael said, "Do you know why you reacted like you did? Why you freed Ben and attacked Tyler?"

She'd prepared for the question. "I wish I did. It had been such a great morning, meeting you and finally feeling like I could relax. I think maybe I let my guard down too far. I felt really good for the first time, and I think when I found the room where that man was tied up, it all hit me in a rush."

"Julian said you were okay at the start."

"Yeah, it was weird. Something came over me and at first I started interrogating him. I wanted to protect Dad and make him proud. But then I had the knife in my hand and I freaked out."

"And helped him escape."

"I know," Eva moaned. "It was so horrible."

"Do you know where that man is now?"

She scoffed. "I wish I did. I'd gladly hand him back. Once we were free of the house, he was gone. He left me stranded, and I was too terrified to go home."

"You could have gone back, you know. He would have understood. You've made things worse by running away."

Eva moaned again. "I've screwed up so bad. I can't even imagine how mad he must be at me. How can he ever trust me again after that? How can I ever trust me again after that?"

"I've known your dad for a long time and I can assure you, he will understand. Come into my office and have a drink. Once you've settled, we can call him."

"I don't think I can do that."

"Let me call him."

"But——"

"I won't tell him you're here. I'll feel him out and see what his head space is like. I'll tell him I spoke to you and tell him exactly what you told me."

"Then what?"

"We can take things slow. If you're not ready, you can stay with me for a while."

"Really? You'd do that for me?"

"I'd do anything for you, Eva."

"Thank you."

Eva followed him down the hall, passing the second door on the left. "Wait." She stopped and took a step back.

"What?"

She pointed at her door. "Why does that feel familiar?" It didn't at all.

Michael smiled. "That was your office. Bring back any memories?"

"Not really. But do you mind if I go in and have a look around?"

"It's your office. Do you want me to come with you?"

"No. I'd like to go in myself."

"You're pretty upset. I think I should stay with you."

She moved in close to him and pressed her flat hand on his chest. "Why don't you go get that drink, and I'll join you after I have a quick look around. I just need a moment. Just to see if I remember anything."

He put his hand on hers to hold it there. "And what if your memory does comes back?"

"I'll call you. Instantly. I promise. I just need a minute."

"Okay. I'm at the end of the hall when you're ready."

She pulled her hand back, but he kept hold of her fingers and smiled his disarming smile before leaving her. The first time she'd seen it, she melted. Now it was only irritating.

She waited until he'd gone into his office before she went into hers, looking around as she made her way to the chair behind the desk. Nothing was familiar, but it looked like they hadn't touched her stuff since she left.

She opened the top drawer and found it a mess. Judging by how tidy the rest of her office was, it looked like someone had been through her things after all. If someone had found the list, they'd have nothing.

She glanced up at the door before reaching around the drawer, searching for a hidden compartment, but she couldn't find anything. She tried the second drawer and still nothing. Pushing back the chair, she looked at the desk, then got to her knees and looked up underneath. She ran her hand along the bottom, but still found nothing.

After getting back up onto the chair, she leaned back and closed her eyes, trying to slow her pounding heart. If she had told Lynn about a secret compartment, then there must be something here. She just needed a hint about where to look.

Tipping her head sideways, she noticed a thin drawer across the front of the desk. It wasn't a hidden drawer, but it wasn't easily seen either. She pulled it open and found pens and markers, but when she slid her hand in, she found a gap at the top of the drawer and inside was a file she slid out. She flipped through the pages to confirm it was what she was looking for, then she folded the file and tucked it into the back of her pants, pulling her jacket over the top. Now she needed to come up with a way to get out of the building without Michael suspecting anything.

He was sitting on the edge of his desk, looking at his phone when she entered. He lifted his gaze and smiled. "Don't worry, I'm not contacting your dad," he said, lifting his phone. "Just checking my emails."

"I already trust you. You don't have to prove yourself."

"Any memories resurface while you were in there?"

"No. I looked through all the stuff at my desk and couldn't remember anything."

"Were you expecting to? Your memory has been gone for a while now. Do you still think it will return?" He handed her a tumbler.

"I wouldn't mind remembering you a little more." She swirled the liquid around, staring into the contents so she wouldn't have to look him in the eyes.

"I like it better this way. I don't mind getting to impress the girl I like."

She bit her lip. Maybe she'd done too good of a job. He wouldn't want to let her go. "Did I used to drink much?"

"Not a lot. But I'd encourage you to drink up now. It won't help you remember anything, but it might make your mistake easier to bear."

"You know, maybe I should just go see my dad and get it over with. He's been so kind to me. I owe him that."

"You don't want to talk it through?"

"No. You said yourself that he'd understand. Running away was stupid. I need him to know I'm on his side."

"I'm glad you see it that way."

She put the glass down. "I'll go now before I lose my nerve. He's probably worried."

Michael took hold of her hand. "I wouldn't advise that. I'm confident he'll understand, but I don't know what his reaction will be if you turn up unexpectedly. He might act rashly in the moment, and I'd hate for either of you to do anything you'd regret."

"He's been nothing but patient with me. He knows what I've been through. I'll be safe."

"Then stay with me for a little while, anyway. I've missed you. It meant a lot to me you reached out and trusted in me."

Eva's stomach curled. When she imagined being with a man who was loyal to Julian, it made her head spin. She knew Julian had wanted them to get together. That alone made it clear he was dangerous.

"Let me get this out of the way first. Then we can focus on us." She forced herself to take a step closer. He had to be convinced she was no threat.

"If only you knew how in love with me you were. I do miss that."

"I thought you said you liked it better this way."

"I do. I'm trying to make the most of it. But it's still

hard."

"Michael, you promised me the first day we met—met again—you'd be patient. Right now, I have to sort things out with my dad."

"Let me call him first and tell him you're okay."

She pulled back, but he tightened his grip, so she relented. If she gave herself away now, it would escalate things, and she didn't know if she was a better fighter than Michael or not. She also didn't want to escalate things unnecessarily. It would be better to get out of there without Julian being alerted until she was gone.

She squeezed his hand so he'd loosen his grip, then reached up and rested a hand on his neck. "I want this to work. I really do. I'm just not ready yet."

His jaw tightened and he put a hand on her hip. "You're more ready than you think." He pulled her closer, wrapping his arm around her and going in for a kiss, but he stopped when he felt the stiffness in her back.

"What's this?" He pulled the papers from their hiding place and moved them out of her reach as she grabbed for them.

"They're nothing. Just some papers I found in my office."

He looked at them, then looked at her. His head tipped mildly to the side, and she knew she was found out.

Twisting out of his grip, she tried to punch him, but he was ready and she was too close. He grabbed her wrist, then grabbed the glass off the desk and smashed it across her head.

Chapter 12

"I CAN'T DO THIS. I can't sit here waiting." Ben opened the door. The car was suffocating. He still couldn't discern if he was being driven by fear, affection, or something else. It felt like something else, but he couldn't be sure.

"Ben, hang on," Lynn said. "I can see you're agitated, but unless you have a clear go-ahead—not to mention a plan—there's nothing more we can do. You can't get into the office."

"That's what I'm counting on."

"What does that mean?"

"I can't stay here. If I'm not back in a half hour, head back to Clara's."

"Ben, wait."

"I can't."

"Ben."

"Do me a favor and don't stop praying."

He hurried across the road, aware of every car and pedestrian that passed him, but his focus was singular.

The only conclusion he'd come to was that there was no way into the building. He trusted that if God wanted him inside, he'd make a way, and if not, Ben had nothing to lose by being stopped by a locked door.

Okay, God. If you're the driving force here, then show me how to get in. If not, I'll go back to the car with my tail between my legs and admit that I'm too emotionally involved.

When he reached the front door, he yanked on it. It opened.

He only paused for a second while his resolve strengthened. He was right. Eva needed help.

The wall in the lobby showed that the PR company Eva had worked for was on the seventh floor. He rode the elevator up to the sixth floor, then entered the stairwell.

At the seventh-floor door, he found another unlocked door.

"You're almost making this too easy for me," he mumbled up to heaven. "I don't mind a little challenge, but I'm glad to know we're on the same page."

He poked his head through the door far enough to confirm that the hall was empty, then entered the floor and listened. He could hear a man's voice.

"I won't lie to you. I'm disappointed. I thought we had a second chance."

"You never had a first chance." Eva kept her tone casual.

"That is an utter and complete lie. When we met the first time, you couldn't hide your attraction. I saw it. You may have been faking this time, but you weren't then. It's too bad. We would have been the perfect couple."

"It would have been perfect for you, maybe. Not for me."

"Why not?"

Ben closed in on Michael's office. The door was partially open at an angle that didn't make it possible to look inside.

"Because," Eva said, "you believe in what Julian stands for and I don't. I want no part of that."

"That's the reason? I am nothing like him. Sure, I believe in what he's doing and I want to be a part of the ruling party, but we could have been so much more."

"You're not my type."

"Do you even remember what your type is? Have you gotten your memory back after all?"

"I don't need it."

"I can't say I believe you. What are these names you've got listed here?"

"I told you, they're nothing. I could remember keeping a list of people I had information on. I wanted to see that list in case it stirred my memory."

"And did it?"

"No."

Michael shook his head. "I'm sorry, Eva, but you're too good. There's no way for me to know the difference, so I'll have to go along with Julian's orders."

"And what are those?"

"To kill you. Once that's done, it will be easier to move on."

"You think Julian will be happy with you murdering his daughter?"

"Eva, the only reason you're not dead already is

because Julian believed you lost your memory. Now, you're only good to him dead. That's what he said to me if you ever contacted me. I wanted to keep you alive, but it's clear Julian was right."

"Fine, then kill me already."

Ben's stomach tightened. He put his hand on the door.

"You're in a hurry," Michael said.

"I'm not a fan of delaying the inevitable."

"And yet you were attempting to delay the inevitability of Julian's rise in power."

"You really do love the sound of your own voice, don't you?"

"It's the only reasonable one in the room."

"Julian will never reach the heights he's aiming for. He can't."

"You think his goals are too lofty?"

"I think he thinks too much of himself. But you can find out for yourself."

"If you're dead, who will be left to stop him?"

"God."

Michael laughed. "I can't tell whether you're serious or not."

"I'm about to die. I have no reason to lie."

"I think that knock on your head has made you delusional."

"You can think what you want. Doesn't matter to me one way or the other."

"You really have no interest in saving yourself?"

"Nope."

"Such a waste. I really hate waste. I don't know what

you thought you would accomplish coming in here on your own."

Ben charged into the room. "She's not on her own." He swung at Michael when he turned.

Michael dropped to the floor, then rolled away and got to his feet, but by the time he stood, Ben had the gun pointed at him.

"Don't know why you didn't just lead with the gun," Michael said, looking amused. "So who's your friend, Eva?"

"I'm Ben."

"No kidding? *The* Ben? I've heard so much about you. Is it true that you blew yourself up to stop Julian?"

"Do I look blown up?" He moved over to Eva. Blood covered the side of her face and soaked her shirt.

"How'd you get in here?" she asked as he untied her from the chair.

"The door was open. You okay?" There was a gash near her eyebrow. "You haven't lost too much blood?"

"I'll live."

"Good. You think you can tie Michael to the chair?"

"Wait. The papers." Eva walked over to Michael, who looked bored. She pushed aside his suit jacket and took the file.

"So it was the two of you all along?" Michael said. "How did you get in here?"

"It was like I told Eva. The door was unlocked."

"Fine, don't tell me. At least now I know why Eva had a change of heart. I don't know if she told you this, Ben, but she had it bad for me not that long ago. Don't be surprised if she changes her mind again once she's finished with you. She's always been finicky. It won't take her long to lose interest."

"Does saying that make you feel better?" Ben stepped closer.

"Ben, forget him. He's stalling," Eva said, pushing him back. "We've gotta get out of here. Now."

"We will, but we need to tie him up first."

She swiped the gun from Ben. "We don't have time for that."

He reached out to stop her as she swung her arm around and hammered it against Michael's head. He fell to the ground.

Eva looked down at his unconscious body to make sure he wasn't getting back up, then looked at Ben. "Julian will be—what's wrong?"

"Nothing. I thought you were going to kill him."

"Would that have been so bad?" Her face fell.

"That's not what I meant."

"But I am a killer. You and I both know that."

"He's not dead."

"That's because I don't lack self-control. That doesn't mean I didn't want to." She looked down at Michael. "We have to go. We need to find a way out of here. Michael's already called Julian. He'll be here any second."

"God got me in. He can get us out."

"Then you better lead out. You've got more faith than me on this one."

They hurried out of the office and he led Eva toward the stairwell where he'd entered, but when he put his hand on the door, he felt a warning. He turned to her. "We can't go out this way."

"Why not?"

"Trust me. Let's try the elevator."

But when they reached the elevators, he sensed the same internal alarm. "Can't go this way either."

"There's no other way out."

He looked around him, then pointed down the hall. "That way."

They entered an office, and both surveyed the space.

Eva went to the window, looking for a latch. "It doesn't open."

"Probably don't want it to. I don't imagine there's a way down from the seventh floor besides a free fall."

"Then I guess our only choice is how we die, because unless there's some secret exit in here, we're trapped. Julian will know we didn't have time to get out, and they'll come looking for us. I really thought we were going to get out of this for a moment. But we've hit a dead end."

"We have to remember all the things God has done for us so far."

"I do."

"Then why are you making this difficult?"

"What? I'm not making anything difficult. We're trapped. That's reality. If you want to pretend like God will open a magic hole in the wall and walk us outside, fine, but I don't know him like that, remember? I'm doing my best. You find it easy to trust him in crazy ways. I struggle."

"You said you wanted me to lead the way because I have the faith, so let me lead."

Eva wanted to respond with an angry retort, but she had nothing, so she threw her arms up and paced the room. "Fine. Lead. What do we do?"

She hadn't been completely honest with Ben. God wasn't the one she didn't trust. It was Ben. Enough had happened that she couldn't deny that God was real, but she didn't like the fact that God talked to him and not to her.

She tried to pray while she walked from one side of the room to the other, but the knock to her head made her fuzzy. She pressed her fingers against the cut on her head. It was still bleeding.

"Hey," Ben said. "I'm sorry if I've upset you."

"Don't worry about it. This will all be over soon."

"That cut looks bad. We should try to wrap your head in something."

"Why? What difference will it—"

Shouts erupted in the hall and he grabbed Eva, pulling her around the desk where they dropped to hide underneath it.

She pressed close to him so she could whisper in his ear. "You don't think this is another one of those times when we're supposed to give ourselves to the enemy, like what you did when Tyler came for you?"

"I won't do that unless we have no other choice. Is that what you're thinking?"

"No, not at all. I've got nothing."

The door opened silently and light from the hall reached their hiding spot.

Eva shifted to get into position so she could fight back when they were discovered. If they were going to die tonight, she planned on making it as difficult as possible for them. She looked at Ben and gave him a quick nod that she was ready. He did the same.

Chapter 13

THE OFFICE CHAIR in front of Ben and Eva moved away from the desk and a figure leaned down. Eva's foot kicked out and should have planted on the man's face. If she'd had more time to process the unexpected outcome of her kick, she probably would have backed away. Instead, she pulled her leg in and quickly shifted to lunge toward the intruder, but Ben dove in the small space and wrapped his arms around her waist, pinning her to the side of the desk.

"Don't," he grunted as she fought to get loose. "Wait."

"What—" Her words halted when she realized the newcomer remained crouched a few feet away with his hands clasped in front of him. He was watching. Amused. She stopped straining and Ben let go. When the stranger didn't make a move, she looked at Ben. "What is this? What's going on?"

"He's a friend."

"Hi, Eva. I'm Felix. It's nice to formally meet you."

He held out his hand with a warm smile that didn't fit the surroundings.

She looked at the offered handshake but didn't reciprocate. "You can't be a friend."

Felix pulled his hand back, looking completely unfazed at her snub. "You're wondering how I got in here without being seen by those guys out there who are trying to find and kill you?"

"I—Yes. That's exactly what I'm wondering."

"I'm good at picking my timing. Aren't I, Ben?"

"He's the best. But, Felix, I sure hope you're here to help get us out."

"I am. Things are delicate at the moment."

"I thought I felt God's leading to come in here. The doors were open when I entered the building. But when we tried to leave, I didn't think it was safe."

"There have been complications."

"What does that mean?"

"It means you're going to have to trust me. It was easier for me to come in and pull you out, rather than let you keep moving forward on your own."

"Hang on," Eva interrupted. "What am I missing? Is Felix some sort of special agent or something?"

Ben looked at Felix and shrugged with one shoulder. "He's an angel."

Eva's face was deadpan. "What?"

"She doesn't believe you." The same amused smile rested comfortably on Felix's face.

"No, I don't believe him. You're wearing a plaid shirt and jeans."

"Should I have changed?" Felix said, plucking at the shirt.

"He's been wearing the same thing for weeks," Ben said.

Eva reached out and poked Felix in the shoulder. "He's a person."

"No, I'm not."

"Is this a joke? 'Cause it's really not funny. There are men out there who will kill us if they find us, and it's probably only seconds until they come looking in here."

Felix shook his head. "We still have a few minutes. But the bottom line is, I wouldn't be here if I weren't confident both of you would follow. So we can go anytime."

"Are you serious?"

"He is. Is he right or wrong?"

Before Eva could respond, Felix said, "Ready to go?" He didn't bother to wait for a response before walking to the door.

Ben waited behind him, but Eva struggled with her own stubbornness. If it hadn't been for her bleeding head and the absurdity of it all, she may have stayed put just to prove something not worth proving. But in the end, she joined the other two.

"If this is going to work," Felix whispered back to them, "you both need to do what I say when I say it. We're not going to have a conversation about the merits of my decision making."

"Does that mean you won't be magically transporting us down to the street?" Ben said with a hopeful grimace.

"Not this time. Follow me exactly. Got it?"

Ben nodded, but Felix wasn't looking at him.

Eva gritted her teeth but then said, "Yeah."

"Good. And don't forget, if you choose to rebel, that is your choice, but be prepared for the consequences."

"I said I got it. Can we just get out of here?"

Felix's steady look shifted to the cut over her eye. "That's still bleeding."

She put a hand to it. "I think so, yeah."

"It would be better if it weren't. You're struggling to focus because of the head knock and the blood loss. Ben?" He looked at Ben expectantly.

"What?"

"She has a wound that needs seeing to."

"Oh right. Uh…" He took off his jacket. "I guess I can tear my shirt up to use as a bandage. I would have done it sooner—"

"That's not what I meant," Felix said.

"It's not?" Ben looked around for another answer.

"Do you remember the job you did outside Afghanistan?"

"Which one?"

"The one where Sergeant Matthews got shot in the stomach."

"Oh…wait, you mean—"

"I do."

"Will that work?"

"How will you know unless you try?"

He looked at the door. "Do we have time?"

"You're stalling."

"No—" He squirmed. "Maybe."

"We have time."

"What is he talking about?" Eva said.

Ben bit the inside of his lip, then reached up a hand toward her. "May I?"

Her head jerked back. "May you what?"

He glanced at Felix. "It didn't feel this stupid then."

"That's because Sergeant Matthews was about to die. And you shouldn't feel stupid now. It's important. Go on."

Ben sighed and looked sheepishly at Eva. "I'm going to pray for healing."

"I really didn't think this evening could get any more weird. You're serious?"

"Yeah."

"Why doesn't he do it?" She bobbed her head toward Felix. "He's the angel."

Felix smirked. "Except you don't really believe I am."

"Does that diminish your power or something?"

"She has exceptional sarcasm in the face of danger, Ben. You should be impressed."

"I'm not. Look, Eva, I don't have to do this."

"Would you prefer if it was me?" Felix asked.

Judging by the look on Felix's face, Eva assumed he already knew her answer, but she said it anyway. "I'd rather Ben, thanks." Her strength was draining away, so she had nothing to lose. She stepped toward Ben and closed her eyes.

"Uh, okay. So, this is awkward, but——" Ben put a hand on her head and blew out a breath toward the floor. "God, I ask that Eva's cut would stop bleeding, that her blood pressure would remain normal, and we can all get out of here safely."

"Amen," Felix said.

Eva opened one eye. "That's it? That's how you heal people?"

"It's not a formula. Ben prayed from his heart."

"So you just pray from your heart and everyone gets healed?"

"That's not how it works either."

"Then how does it work?"

"If you want to learn about healing, you need to ask *Him*."

"Who?"

"God," Ben said.

"Listen, guys, I appreciate all of this, and I do believe God does some amazing things. He's done a lot for me in a short time, but this whole healing thing is pushing it for me."

"I know," Felix said. "How's your head?"

"It hurt—" She hadn't noticed the moment when her raging headache had disappeared. She reached for her forehead, her fingers prodding through the sticky blood. The cut was gone. "That's impossible."

"All right, you two, it's time to go."

"But—"

"Eva, that was a gift. Now's the time when you have to trust me."

He opened the door and walked out into the hall without checking to see that it was clear. Ben followed, but Eva faltered. Everything was moving too fast. This God stuff was new territory for her. But she couldn't risk being left behind, so she reached out and took hold of Ben's jacket, allowing his momentum to drag her into the abyss of the unknown.

She scouted the hall when she entered, even though it would have been too late. It was clear.

Felix led them into the stairwell and trotted down two floors before entering the door to the fifth level. After Ben and Eva were through, he closed the door and waited.

"This will only be a moment," he whispered.

They could hear the muffled footsteps of a group going up.

"They've already checked this floor," Felix said before opening the door and heading farther downstairs.

When they were on the second floor, he moved them onto the level and waited again. This time longer.

They heard the voices of the passing party, then Felix led them to the ground floor.

"You need to follow directly behind me. Directly." He looked them both in the eye and waited for them to acknowledge his command.

Once he was satisfied he had their cooperation, he pulled the door open and Ben and Eva moved into position at Felix's back.

Eva clung to Ben as they moved out into the foyer and across the room. She stopped breathing and almost staggered when she saw the two armed men standing guard at the door. Now her instincts were firing. She battled with her will in order to keep step with Ben when everything inside her threatened mutiny. Her mind screamed at her to fight or take cover, but she kept her feet in time with Ben's and didn't miss a step.

Felix skirted the edge of the room. The guards didn't notice their presence. Then he paused twenty feet from the front door and waited.

A squawk came from the guards' walkie-talkies and they moved toward the elevators. Felix strolled forward and out the front door that was left unattended.

Once they were outside, Felix ushered Ben and Eva in front of him. "Walk in a straight line to the end of the block, then turn left."

Eva kept close to Ben's back until they turned the corner and stopped, waiting for further instructions.

"That's it, folks. You're clear," Felix said with a generous smile.

Eva looked back the way they came. "You're invisible?"

"Hang on," Ben said. "You told me others could see you."

"They can. If those two guards had looked directly at me, they would have seen me. Otherwise, I go unnoticed."

"And what if they had looked at you?"

"They weren't going to."

"Whatever happened back there," Eva said, "we wouldn't have gotten out if it weren't for you. Thank you."

Felix took hold of Eva's hand. "Remember what happened today. You need to be bold in trusting Him. Let tonight be a lesson for you. Both of you."

"I won't ever forget," Eva said. She was confused by Felix's sad smile. "You don't believe me?"

"You'd be surprised what people forget when they don't actively remember. You need to continue seeking Him and remember what He has done, or else you will forget. I've seen it too many times."

"You're talking about the Israelites?" Ben said.

"I don't have to go back nearly that far."

"I guess humanity doesn't hold too much surprise for you these days."

"Not often, but it does happen. When people give themselves fully over to the One who loves them most, there are always surprises to be had."

"We should get going," Ben said. "We can't stick around here too long, but I didn't see Lynn out the front with the car."

Ben and Eva looked back up the street.

"She must have moved when Julian's guys turned up," Eva said.

"I told her to go back to Clara's if we didn't come out in time."

"No. I don't know how I know, but I don't believe she'd leave us here. She'll be here somewhere." Eva turned back to Ben. "Where's Felix?"

Ben looked behind him and sighed. "He does that."

"So, he really was an angel?"

"Yeah."

"Is it normal to meet one like a regular person?"

"I wouldn't call that regular."

"Do you see him often?"

"At the moment? Yeah. I've seen him a few times recently. Whatever we're in the middle of must be big. But he's the only one, and it only started the day I nearly died."

"Well, we'd better find Lynn and get out of here."

"You're covered in blood."

Eva lifted the collar of her shirt and wiped her face. "Not much we can do about it."

"No. You'll have to stay out of sight. I'll see if I can spot Lynn."

Eva stepped toward the wall so she could lean against it, but her legs gave out. Ben wrapped an arm around her waist and lifted her to help her walk. "Whoa. Looks like God kept your blood pressure up while we escaped, but it's dropped again."

"I thought I was healed."

"You were, but you still lost blood and you've had a lot of adrenaline pumping through your body. We need to get you home so you can rest."

A truck approached with its headlights off.

"Lynn," Ben said. "Thank you, God."

Ben slid Eva into the back seat.

"What happened?" Lynn said when she saw the blood.

"I'm okay. Just get us out of here."

"I thought I'd lost you both when Julian turned up. I can't believe you got out. I've been praying nonstop."

"Wait until you hear how we were rescued," Eva said.

"That will have to wait," Ben said. "Doctor's orders. You need to rest. I'll drive and, Lynn, I'll fill you in on the way home."

Lynn and Ben swapped seats and Lynn got Eva into position with her head down and feet anchored on the door to keep them up.

"I know you guys have had a big night," Lynn said. "But did we get what we needed?"

"Yeah, I got it." Eva pulled the papers from behind her back and handed them to Lynn. "We got it all. I just hope you can make sense of it."

Lynn looked eagerly through the file. She knew the names, but the codes that were written beside different names meant nothing to her. They'd risked a lot to get this list, but from what she could see, without Eva's memory, they still had nothing.

She looked up at the rearview mirror. Ben's eyes were focused on the road. She didn't have the heart to give him the bad news yet.

Chapter 14

BACK AT CLARA'S, Lynn helped Eva get cleaned up and left her resting in the other room.

"She'll feel better in the morning," Lynn said to Clara and Ben, who were sitting in the kitchen.

"You can leave her where she is," Ben said. "It's too crowded in the bunker. She'll sleep better up here. I'll keep watch while the rest of you get some sleep."

Clara glared at Ben. "Think I'm useless, do ya?"

"No, that's not—"

"I'll stay here and help, if you don't mind. You can't watch every angle all night. And you're no good to us half dead from lack of sleep. You'll need to get some sleep, like the rest of us."

"Okay. You can help. Thank you."

"If you need me to take a turn, let me know," Lynn said.

"We'll be fine." Clara went to the stove to heat some water. "You stay close to Eva in case she needs you. In fact, why don't you put her on my bed? It's a double and you can both sleep there in case she needs you in the night."

"Has she been waking in the night?" Lynn asked.

Ben and Clara looked at each other. "We haven't spoken a word about it, but a couple of times she's had bad dreams. She's never mentioned if she remembers and we haven't asked, but after tonight, there's a fair chance she'll wake sometime tonight. She'll need someone there to calm her."

Lynn nodded. "She never complained about having bad dreams before, but this could be since everything that's happened. She is different, you know. You two wouldn't know it, but she is."

"I like her just fine." Clara lifted her chin in defense.

"I don't mean that to sound critical. I like the change. She was harder before. Determined and single-minded. She's more real now. And softer."

"I guess after what she endured with Julian, she had to be tough. Maybe it is best if she never remembers."

"Yeah." Lynn dipped her head toward the floor to hide the concerned crease that appeared on her forehead. "I'm going to get some sleep. Call me if you need me."

"Lynn," Ben said before she turned.

"Yeah?"

"The list doesn't help us, does it?"

"What?" Clara turned from the stove.

"The list Eva got. We can't use it, can we?"

Lynn licked her lips to buy herself time.

"Hang on a sec," Clara said, pulling the kettle from

the heat when it whistled. "I thought that was all we needed. I thought it had the names."

Lynn's shoulders fell. "It's got all the names, but I can't decipher Eva's code. How'd you know, Ben?"

"I'm good at reading people. Does Eva know?"

"I didn't tell her yet."

"Didn't tell me what?" Eva said from the door.

"You should be resting," Ben said.

"I'm fine. I heard the kettle and thought I'd like a cup. I'm glad I did. What haven't you told me?"

"I didn't want you to worry," Lynn said. "It's the list. I don't know what to do with it. I don't know how to use it."

Eva leaned back against the wall. "So all of that was for nothing."

"Not nothing. It's never for nothing," Lynn said.

"Why would Felix even bother saving us? We all agreed I should go, but it's all for nothing. Every time we think we get ahead, it turns out we're further back than when we started. It's impossible."

"It can't be for nothing," Lynn said. "You used to remind me all the time that nothing is impossible for God."

"*I* used to say that?"

"Yeah."

"So I was a Christian?"

"I was with you when you gave your life to Jesus."

"I wish I could remember that. Any bits of memory that have come back have been filled with violence. And here you are, the only hope I have, and I never even asked you how we met."

"There have been more pressing matters."

"Not anymore. We're at a dead end. Were we friends from the start?"

"No. Not until you almost killed me."

If it hadn't been for the smile on Lynn's face, Eva would have fallen apart. The hopelessness of the situation and exhaustion from the night was getting to her.

"Here I was thinking I'd get a good memory."

"It is a good memory. Trust me."

"I'd love to hear it," Ben said.

"I'd have to start from the beginning. Are you up for that?"

"Sure."

"Okay. The church I go to in DC is full of people who work in politics. A few of us started talking, and it became clear that we all had the same concern. An organization called the Underwood Foundation was getting a lot of press and the media was talking about the guy who ran it. A man named Julian. They made him out to be some kind of saint, but something about him didn't sit right. We thought we needed to do something, so we prayed together about it. At the beginning, it was mostly a general sense that something was building. But the more we learned about Julian Underwood, the harder we prayed."

"So this all started as a small group at your church?" Ben said.

"Wow," Clara chimed in. "Guess the muddy water of the Underwood Foundation went deeper than you expected."

"No kidding." Lynn shook her head. "Honestly, I

didn't expect it to go beyond prayer. We had programs at the church to help the homeless and single parents, and I'd volunteer for that stuff. It's easy to help when it doesn't cost you much besides a bit of time and a dip into your pocket now and then."

"When did things change?"

"Our church began raising money for persecuted Christians in other nations. We were told stories of what churches with no freedom of religion were dealing with. I thought I was being noble, celebrating the freedom we had here."

"There's nothing wrong with that."

"I know, and you're right. There isn't. But it's about what happened next. One Sunday morning while someone was listing off the announcements, out of nowhere, God asked me if I was willing to risk my life for him. Would I put myself on the line like the people we were hearing about?"

"Wow. You obviously said yes."

"No way. Not at first. I thought he was asking me to move to one of those countries we'd heard about. I refused. I liked my job and my life. I acquiesced that I wasn't strong enough to stand up for my faith like those people. I thought that was it. I thought—or rather, hoped—all God was trying to do was highlight my weakness."

"It never occurred to you he meant for you to risk your life at home?"

She looked at the other three in the room. "I'm not like you guys. My homelife was normal growing up. I grew up in church, I got good grades, went to a good university, and ended up at the White House because I'm interested in economics and politics. My life has always been safe and ordered. I've never even been in a car accident."

Eva joined them at the table. She clasped her hands and rested them on the table. With her head bowed, it looked like she was praying. "That's all the things I thought I wanted. To be normal. But even you aren't safe from it."

"None of us are, really. There are a lot of people who will be impacted by Julian and they don't know it. God hasn't called them, but he's called us. I don't know why. If I try to make sense of it, I go crazy."

"But what made you change your mind?"

"I wasn't sleeping well, and I've always been a good sleeper. I couldn't stop thinking that God hadn't been satisfied with my answer. It got so bad I had to tell the group I was praying with. Turns out we had all been convicted in a similar way. I can see why God wants us to be in fellowship with one another. I wouldn't have done any of this without their support."

Clara cleared her throat. "Just wonderin' what God said to you all when you prayed."

"At first nothing. I think we were all secretly hoping God hadn't meant it. Or that at the very worst, he was asking us to tell people on the street that Jesus loved them. Embarrass ourselves a little maybe, but nothing more. That's when I saw a news report about Julian and the charity work he'd been doing for vulnerable kids. The footage they showed was at a charity ball you attended with him, Eva. As soon as I saw your face, I knew."

"Knew what?"

"That I had to get close to you somehow. I didn't even know why."

"But how? How could you know something like that so certainly?"

"I can't explain it any better than I just knew. Looking back on it, it seems nuts. God had to have been in it because I never would have done it on my own. I took time off work—which I never do—and got a job as an intern at your PR firm to try to get close to you."

Eva shook her head. "Did you have any idea how dangerous that was?"

"Not really. Not at first. If I had known you were going to try to kill me, I never would have done it."

"How did I find out who you were?"

"You looked into my credentials and discovered I was way overqualified."

"How did you stop me from killing you?"

"I didn't. I have no doubt you would have done it if God hadn't already been working on you."

"Is that what I said?"

"Not in so many words, but it was obvious."

"Obvious how?"

Lynn's eyes dropped to the table. "It doesn't matter. You made a decision to follow Jesus in the end and that's what counts."

Eva's cheek twitched as she clenched her teeth. She would have preferred to keep her teeth together and not ask the question that terrified her. But she had to know.

"Please. If I get my memory back one day, I'd like to be prepared for what's coming."

Lynn looked at the other two in the room. "We should go somewhere private."

"No." Eva shook her head emphatically. "I'm not going to hide who I was, or pretend that person didn't exist. Especially not to these two. They've risked their lives for me. They deserve to know."

"You're sure?"

"I am."

Lynn's fingers twisted around each other. "Julian was trying to procure the help of a bank CEO. You discovered some activities he was involved in and Julian wanted you to use that knowledge to get his cooperation."

"Blackmail." Eva let out a tiny sigh of relief. "I'm not surprised by that at all. I've figured out that much about myself." Eva snuck a look at Ben. He didn't look surprised either.

"Not blackmail," Lynn said, drawing Eva's attention back to her.

"What else is there?"

"Eva, you need to understand that Julian had a power over you before you were saved. Jesus set you free. I saw it happen. It was miraculous. But Julian raised you, and for a time...he owned you. He had a way of making you do what he wanted. I haven't known you for a long time, but I've known you long enough to be certain of that."

"What did I do?" Eva's voice was hoarse.

"You really don't need—"

"Tell me."

"You gave the CEO what he wanted."

"What did he want?" The question spilled from her mouth before she could stop it.

Lynn cleared her throat. "A kid."

"You mean like…" The words dissolved at the expressionless look on Lynn's face.

Eva's arms wrapped around herself as her stomach revolted. "How can I ever—"

"Because you've been forgiven."

"No. Not for that. I could never be forgiven for that."

"You did save the boy in the end."

"And that makes it okay?" She turned and stumbled out the door. "I need some—I don't know."

Chapter 15

BEN'S HAND CRAMPED, but his tight fist was the only thing keeping the lump in his throat from roaring out as a scream while he stared out the door where Eva had disappeared into the dark. His heart broke for her. He had held out hope that she had nothing too horrifying to regret from her past. He had been confident she wasn't as bad as she thought, but he was wrong. She was the thing she had feared the most, and he couldn't ignore his own revulsion at her actions. But Lynn was right. God had changed Eva's heart. It took something monstrous for her to hit rock bottom, but it's what saved her in the end. There had to be a way to help her to understand that.

Felix's recent words forced into his mind. The angel had been adamant that Ben was not the one to fix her. That was God's job. But that didn't stop him from feeling desperate to help. It couldn't be right for him to sit on his hands and do nothing. He couldn't stand by and let her hurt like that.

"I shouldn't have told her," Lynn said, pacing the floor.

Ben released his fists and turned to her. "You had to. She was bound to find out one day, and it's what she wanted."

Clara cleared her throat. "I'm just happy to hear I'm not the only freak of the lot." She swiped away a wet smudge on her cheek and disappeared down the hall.

"Is she okay?" Lynn said after Clara left the room.

"We all have our demons to face."

"I can't help but feel I've made a mess of everything."

"You already knew the truth and you've had time to process it. It's going to take the rest of us some time too."

"What about you?"

"What about me?"

"I know you respected Eva before. I hope I didn't change that. She is a good woman."

"I know. I should see if she's okay."

"Maybe you should give her some space."

"I can't. Maybe I should, but I can't leave her with that. She needs to know that I—that we don't despise her." He headed into the dark, arguing away Felix's warning.

Her outline was barely visible near the edge of the woods.

"Eva."

"Don't," she said without turning.

"You can't torture yourself over that."

"Yes, I can. I deserve——" Her throat closed around her words.

"You heard Lynn. Julian has a way of making people do things against their will. Even I know that."

"Oh yeah?" She turned. "Did he make you get a child for some sick—I told Clara she can't be held responsible for Franky's actions, so how can I now decide that Julian has to be responsible for mine?"

"That's different and you know it."

"Is it?"

"Yes."

"Just leave me alone."

"I can't do that."

"Ben, you're not thinking straight. You heard what I've done. I warned you I was a monster. You didn't believe me, but I was right."

"When I first met your dad——"

"Don't call him that."

"Sorry. Julian. He told me he wanted to change the world for the better and I believed him. But as I worked with him, he slowly wormed this idea into my head that some things are okay to do if it's for the greater good. I agreed with him to a point. I'd been in special forces and had to make difficult choices all the time. It took me a while to see the evil that was really there. He knows how to exploit people. He finds their weaknesses and uses them to get what he wants, and that's what he did to you."

She stepped closer to him, and he wanted to reach out to her. "But there are lines, Ben. Lines that even you would never cross."

"You've got those lines too. You crossed over, but then you realized what you did and you made it right. It's why God could finally get through to you. Once you saw the evil for real, you understood the truth."

"Oh yeah? And what truth is that?"

"That God sees value in you and wants you on his side. He's obviously not done with you yet."

"Oh, I'm pretty sure he is. Or if he isn't, I certainly am."

"Come on, Eva. We've all done bad stuff. Remember that scripture? He'll go to the depths to find you. You used that scripture for a reason."

"There are some places that are too deep, even for him."

"No, there aren't."

"You say that, but you didn't go looking for just the right kid with light hair and freckles."

Ben didn't stop himself reaching for her this time, but when he grabbed her arm, it was to get her to look at him. "Light hair and freckles?" His mouth barely moved as he repeated her description.

Eva's eyes widened and she shivered. Ben reached for her as she fell to the ground, shaking. "No…no… Ben. I can't…no, please. Make it stop." She choked in a breath, then a sobbing bellow came from her throat. He pulled her close as she shuddered. Lynn and Clara ran from the house.

"What in the blazes is going on out here?" Clara called out as she ran. "Ben, what did you do to her? You want to alert the entire state that we're here?"

"Something's wrong," Ben said, pushing the hair off Eva's face. Her forehead was slick with sweat.

Lynn dropped beside her. "Eva, can you hear me?" She gripped Eva's shoulders and began praying under her breath.

"No…" Eva moaned. Her head rolled from side to side.

"It will be okay."

"No, no, NO!" she screamed and tried to throw everyone off her, but Ben held her down.

"Eva," he yelled down at her. "Stop it. You're safe."

She shuddered and stilled. Her eyes blinked up at him, then shifted to Lynn. "Lynnie." Her face twisted.

Lynn looked at Ben, her face pale in the dim light. "She's remembered."

"Remembered what?"

"Oh, Lynnie, I remember everything." Eva curled toward her friend and sobbed into her lap.

Lynn held her tightly and spoke to Ben and Clara. "Can you give us a minute? But stay close. We'll need to bring her inside."

Ben and Clara nodded and stepped back.

Ben paced across the lawn. His pants were wet with the heavy dew that coated the ground. Lynn was right. They needed to get Eva inside. She needed to stay warm. The torment she'd be going through would sap all of her strength.

He rubbed a hand across his chest where it ached. He wanted to go to her. He wanted to save her. Felix had said he couldn't fix her, but he yearned to. More than anything.

When Lynn called to him, he ran.

"Can you lift her?" she said, making room for him.

"Of course." He leaned down and scooped Eva up. Holding her as close as he could, he whispered against her hair, "It'll be okay. Everything is going to be okay."

She clutched his shirt and the tremble that shook her body diminished as he squeezed her to his chest.

Clara led them to her bedroom. "Lay her on my bed. I want her to be as comfortable as we can make her."

Ben slid his arm slowly from under her back as he laid her down. Her fingers still clutched his shirt, so he pressed his hand over hers before sliding his thumb under her fingers to release them. He didn't want to be free of her, but when he was, he brushed her hair from her face before making room for Lynn to sit beside her. He would have curled up beside her himself and wrapped her up in a cocoon if he could have.

Lynn rested a hand on Eva's leg and studied her face before looking up at Ben. "She'll be okay. That's a lot to remember all at once."

"She was afraid of turning back into the person she used to be if she remembered."

Lynn shook her head. "She'll be okay. She's strong. Stronger than all of us, probably. If she remembers me, then she remembers God, and that's the best thing for her right now."

As he backed out of the room, his anger for Julian settled into an ache much colder. A hatred formed a knot in his stomach that he took a moment to revel in. He knew what hatred could do to a person, but it was hard not to protect the feeling. It was vile, yet strangely alluring. Finally, he had to push it aside to keep from punching the wall.

"Call me if you need anything," he said to Lynn before leaving the room.

Clara harrumphed when he entered the kitchen. She was standing at the door, already keeping watch. As frustrating as she could be, she was also fiercely loyal, and Eva needed as many allies as possible right now. He was understanding better what had drawn Eva back to this place, even after what Clara and Franky had done to her.

He went to the stove and made a cup of tea before joining Clara at the door. "Would you mind if I took the first watch?" he said, handing her the steaming cup.

She took it but eyeballed the contents before giving it a sniff. "You didn't put anything in it?"

"You mean besides arsenic?"

"Sugar."

"I would sooner poison it than put sugar in there. You've made it abundantly clear that sweet tea is an abomination."

She took a sip. "It'll do." She handed him the rifle, then went back inside.

He dropped to the porch step and leaned the gun next to him before putting his face in his hands. He didn't think there was a need to watch. If someone was going to come looking for them, they would have already. But it made him feel better to be doing something.

A warm breeze brushed the back of his neck. This time he was prepared when Felix spoke.

"She'll be okay."

Ben looked up at the angel. "Thank you for coming."

"My goodness."

"What?"

"That's the first time you've spoken of an appreciation for my presence."

"That's not true. I'm just not always good at realizing it in time."

"You're growing."

"I sure hope so. Can I assume we're safe here?"

"For now. But stay vigilant."

"I was hoping you *wouldn't* say something like that."

"Right now, you must always stay vigilant. And you must keep your guard up against your feelings as much as anything."

"Are you saying I shouldn't feel bad for her?"

"Is that what you're feeling?"

Ben clicked his tongue. "Why do you do that?"

"What? See through to the heart of the matter?"

"You want me to admit that I care about her?"

"You're allowed to."

"What?"

"Caring about her is not what I warned you about."

"So I'm supposed to do nothing?"

"That's not what I said either."

Ben rubbed his eyes. "It can't be easy for her, discovering that her worst nightmare is real. I can't even begin to imagine what Julian put her through."

"Don't forget that she's not alone."

"I know. It's good that Lynn is here."

"That's not what I meant. He's close to her. He's healing her memories right now."

Ben shook his head. "Everything is so different from what I thought at the beginning."

"Are you trying to say you were wrong?"

"Are you patronizing me?"

"A little. But it's good when you can admit you were wrong. It's the first step."

"Yes, fine. I was wrong. I think back to before and I can't believe I questioned God about why he would want to save Eva."

Felix lowered his head so he was looking at Ben from under his eyebrows. "You think He wouldn't have saved her if she weren't on His side?"

"That's not what I meant."

"Yes, it was."

"Right." He looked out into the dark. "Disagreeing with an angel was a stupid thing to do."

"You're allowed to be stupid now and then."

"That's generous of you."

"But that's not the only thing you're being stupid about."

A laugh slipped from Ben's throat. "I take it you can't wait to enlighten me?"

"I don't have to if you'd rather not know."

"No, please. Let's get this taken care of now."

"Clara."

"What about her?"

"You're not sure what to make of her."

"Can you blame me?"

"She's different from you, but that's not a bad thing."

"I know. I've warmed up to her."

"You've warmed up to the fact that she looks out for Eva, which is in your best interest, but you still don't completely trust her. And you don't see her as part of the family. Believe it or not, she loves her Heavenly Father. She's just got baggage like everyone else."

"She did almost kill Eva the first time they met."

"Should we talk about all the things godly men and women have done over the centuries that have been far worse? Should we discuss the things you've done over the course of your life?"

"But this is different."

"Why?"

"You say she's part of the family, that she's a Christian, but the things Clara believes and the things that I believe don't always match up."

"I hate to tell you, but some of the stuff you think you have all figured out about Him is wrong."

"Like what?"

Felix laughed. "That is not part of my assignment on this visit. Just stick close to Him and keep listening. He'll fill you in as you go. Clara is doing the same. You're in two different places on the journey, but you're both headed in the same direction."

"He'll fill us in as we go...Does that mean ignorance is bliss?"

"There is an allowance for ignorance, but maturity is about a decrease in ignorance and making sure you're continually asking for His wisdom. Make sure you keep listening and respond appropriately when you receive it."

"And what if I make a mistake?"

"Let me set your mind at ease."

"I'd appreciate it."

"You will make a lot of mistakes."

"That's supposed to put my mind at ease?" Ben leaned back onto his elbows. "I guess I already knew that. So what now?" He turned to Felix, but the angel was gone.

It didn't matter. He already knew what he needed to do next.

After shoving up off the step, he went into the house, where he found Clara at the kitchen table. He sat down.

"You done with your watch already?" She grinned. "You army boys are so soft."

"We're safe at the moment."

"How can you possibly know that?" He could see by the look on her face that she was genuinely curious.

"Because I do, but I'm not in here because I'm finished with my watch. I'm in here because I wanted to apologize."

"What for?"

"I misunderstood you. I made assumptions and I was wrong."

She squinted. "Are you bein' serious?"

"Yeah."

"Well then...Can't say I blame ya." She shifted uncomfortably in her seat. "I've made some stupid decisions."

"You have, but so have I. We'll never succeed if we aren't in this together. We're on the same team and we serve the same God."

"Yes, we do."

"How about we start fresh?"

"If it'll get you to stop with all this mushy stuff, I'm in. But I do have one condition."

"Of course you do."

"I want to know if there are aliens at Area 51." Ben licked his lips and Clara cackled. "I'm only teasing you. You wouldn't know, anyway."

Ben shook his head as he stood. "I'm going to turn all the lights out so we're less conspicuous. We'll use those small flashlights if we need to, but otherwise we should stay in the dark."

"I thought you said we were safe?"

"That doesn't mean we don't stay vigilant."

"Good idea."

Ben flicked off the light in the kitchen, then went to Clara's room, where he found Lynn and Eva asleep next to each other on the bed. He leaned on the doorframe and took in the peace of the scene. They had so little of it right now. He sent up a silent prayer, thanking God that they had found Lynn. If she hadn't been here to look after Eva, he didn't know what they would have done.

He turned the light off in the room, then ran his hand along the wall as he made his way back to the kitchen.

"You should close your eyes for a bit," he said to Clara. "I'll wake you when I'm ready for a break."

"Sounds good to me. I'll be in the first bedroom when you're ready to swap."

She started down the hall, and Ben called after her. "Don't forget, you can use the flashlight if you need to."

"Don't need it. I know my way around here with my eyes closed."

He went to the front door and heard a bang as she bumped into something.

"Jesus, Mary and Joseph," came her muffled reply. "Who put that chair there?"

He laughed, then settled himself in the porch chair, ready for a long night.

Chapter 16

EVA HAD to rub at her eyes to get them to open. She rolled onto her back, her body aching from last night's trauma that had settled into a dull ache at the base of her skull. Then she smelled coffee and sat up, breathing deeply.

Lynn was curled up against the wall, still sleeping, when Eva stood. She watched her friend with a mixture of familiarity and confusion. Lynn was one of the few people who knew Eva's darkest secrets, but she could still remember seeing her friend a day ago and not recognizing her. The woman who had saved her from Julian and who had become a best friend had been a stranger yesterday. But Eva also knew God had brought her back at the right time. If it hadn't been for Lynn's whispered prayers throughout the night, Eva would be in much worse shape this morning. The memories had come like a tidal wave, but had eased into a weight more bearable as the night went on.

She left Lynn to sleep and went to the kitchen, but

stopped in the door when she saw Ben. He was facing away from her and she had to cling to the doorframe to keep from rushing back to the bedroom.

He now knew the worst of her. It would be better to get this over with when no one else was in the room.

When she cleared her throat, he turned.

"Hey," he said. His eyes cast around the room, unsure where to settle. "Coffee?"

He had carried her inside and she had clung to him —desperate for a safe haven—as a mountain of regret threatened to crush her.

She needed him to understand, but the sharp edges of her past still dug deep, piercing her soul with agony.

Looking out the window to avoid making eye contact, she said, "Yes, thank you." She couldn't deny the monster that had been lying dormant inside her and now Ben couldn't deny it either. She wouldn't hold it against him if he wanted to leave. Or if he wanted her to go.

He offered her a mug. She took it with a weak smile and sat at the table.

"You okay?" Ben said.

She shrugged. "Better than last night, I guess." She twisted the cup around on the table but didn't take a sip.

"Would you like a drink besides coffee?"

"No." She took a drink, then focused on the contents, working up the courage to speak again. "I'm just…I'm sorry."

"For what?"

"I don't know. For who I am?" She looked up at him, her eyes pleading. "I didn't realize how much freedom

God gave to me. I did terrible things that I can never take back, but he helped me stop doing those things." She pressed her hand to her mouth.

Ben frowned and slid his hand across the table toward her but didn't touch her. "I know you're not a horrible person."

She shook her head. "But you don't know. You don't know all of it. You know the worst, but you don't know it all."

"I don't need to. All I need to know is that you're okay now."

"I won't kill you, if that's what you're wondering."

He laughed lightly and slid his hand back, dropping it into his lap. "No. That's not what I'm wondering at all. Eva, you have no enemies here. We all care for you. We're not afraid of you."

"I know...I do *know* that." She sighed. "Where's Clara?"

"Feeding the chickens."

Eva nodded. There was so much more she wanted to say. So much she wanted to apologize for, but it was too much. Ben didn't hate her as she'd feared, but she couldn't process more than that right now. And they had more important matters to talk about.

"I hope you got some sleep last night."

"Some. Clara and I took it in shifts."

"Took what in shifts?"

"We kept watch so we could sleep upstairs, remember?"

"Right." She found a crumb on the table and pushed it around with her fingernail. "If I had known how good it felt to forget, I would have enjoyed it more while I had the time."

"Do you wish you could go back?"

"To what?"

"Not knowing."

She considered the question before responding. "The selfish part of me does."

"How is that selfish?"

"Because my remembering means you can ask the one question I know you've been dying to ask."

"The only question on my mind all night was if you were okay."

"I don't believe you. Your self-control is admirable, but you can't tell me you haven't been thinking about it."

"Okay, the question was there, but it's not the one at the front of my mind. You were very shaken up last night, and I don't want to force you if you're not ready."

"I don't have a choice. I have to be ready. I've got a lot of bad memories, but they're the key to stopping Julian." A wave of grief came out of nowhere and she dropped her head into her hand, squeezing her eyes against the tears.

Ben jumped from his seat and went around to her. "Whoa. You okay? What's wrong?"

His hand pressed into her back. It was more tenderness than she could take. She stood and walked away from him, pushing down on the emotion. She cared about him, and that meant she needed to protect him from her.

"We don't need to talk about it right now," he said. "You're obviously not ready."

"Ben, I'm not a good person." She faced him. "I need you to understand that. Not really. God saved me when I gave my life to him, but that person I was will never really go away."

"But you're on the other side of that now."

"Only because of Jesus. I was right to be worried about hurting you."

"You just said you wouldn't."

"Not now. But if only part of my memory had come back, I would have turned on all of you. If I had only remembered my commitment to Julian, you'd be dead right now. Yes, I'm on the other side of that, but that doesn't mean who I was isn't still a part of me."

"You really believe that?"

"For a long time I was single-minded in my pursuits. I had one goal in mind, and nothing but death would have stopped me from seeing Julian's vision carried out."

Ben held her gaze for a moment. "Maybe. But there's something you're forgetting."

She broke eye contact and looked out the door. "No. There is nothing I've forgotten. I can assure you. That is the person I was. And she didn't disappear just because of Jesus."

"I see it another way. I think Jesus found the woman who was buried under a pile of filth."

"No." Her whole life, she'd trained everything inside her and channeled it toward precision. That's how she grew up. Meeting Jesus had brought a flood of emotions that weren't natural to her. It wasn't who she was. She needed Ben to understand that. He had to remain wary of her. She would only hurt him in the end. Jesus had saved her, but she was broken beyond repair. "Come with me."

"Where?"

"I want to show you something."

Ben followed her across the yard to the barn. She spotted Clara with the chickens, but Clara acted like she didn't see them. Eva had to expect that. Ben had put on a brave face, but they must have been appalled when they found out what she was capable of.

"What's out here?" Ben said.

Eva pulled the knife from where they'd left it the day before. She flipped it up without looking and caught it. "You remember my last throw?"

"I do."

"Stand there." She put a hand on his chest and shoved him against the wall of the shed before moving back out into the yard.

"I hope you're not about to do what I think you are."

"I am. Don't move."

After walking several paces away and with barely a pause, she turned and threw the knife.

Ben blinked when it embedded in the wall an inch above his head. He reached up and touched the handle. "You've improved."

Eva retrieved the knife. "You didn't flinch."

"You told me not to move."

"You'd be safer if you didn't trust in me so much."

He grinned. "If you were planning on impaling with that dagger, flinching wouldn't have saved me."

"But you trusted me."

"You said you were good. You weren't lying. Why shouldn't I trust you?"

"It wasn't that long ago when I wouldn't have hesitated to hit you with that knife. I cut you free at Julian's house, but there were numerous times when I went the other way. Violence is what I was brought up on. I'll do everything I can to stop Julian, but that's as far as I go with you and Clara."

"Why are you saying all of this?"

"Because it's the way things have to be."

"Why?"

"Because it just is."

"I'm not sure what point you were trying to prove with that knife stunt, but it doesn't have anything to do with who you are on the inside."

"Or maybe you don't know me as well as you think you do."

"Can you still remember the time when you had no memory?"

"Yes."

"Do you remember that person you were?"

She leaned toward him and dropped her voice. "I miss her. I wish I could be her. But she's gone now."

"No, Eva. Julian took that girl you were and molded you into who he wanted you to be, but when you lost all of his influence after falling in the river, you got to experience the person you really are. She's still in there. That is the real you."

"I wish I could find comfort in that, but I don't. I forgot how important that scripture was. How much I needed it."

"The Psalm."

"'If I make my bed in Sheol, behold, You are there.' That's where God found me. I was in hell and he came there to get me out."

"And he's working to renew your mind. To change you back into the person he created you to be."

"I can never make up for all the evil I did."

"You don't have to. That's why Jesus hung on the cross."

"He may have forgiven me, but I can never let it go."

"Why?"

"I can't risk it."

"Risk what?"

"Going back. If I forget what I've done, if I ever let myself feel like I'm okay, I could risk losing it all. What if I fall back into it?"

"That's not how it works."

"How do you know? There is no way for you to know that. I want to help God and do whatever I can to stop Julian, but I will never understand why he didn't leave me to my own destruction." A panic built in her chest. "He saved me from a mess I deserved. He gave me a freedom I don't deserve, and I can never repay him for that or ever allow myself to forget what I'm capable of." She sucked in several breaths to calm herself.

"None of us deserves his grace," Ben said quietly.

"Don't brush over my sins like they're ordinary."

"I never said they're ordinary, but sin is sin."

"You think so? You want to know what my response was when I first started feeling bad about what I was doing? I was ashamed. I considered it a weakness."

"Is that when Lynn came along?"

"Yes. It was about that time when I discovered my new intern was not who she said she was. She was a very capable woman in her forties who said she wanted to start over in a new profession, but after looking into her, I knew she was there for another reason and I was going to make her tell me everything."

"What stopped you?"

"Whatever God was doing to me, I had all these new emotions that were foreign to me. They made me afraid. And Lynn was so fearless. If you ask her about it now, she'll say she was terrified, but I couldn't see that. And there was something in her that I could sense but couldn't understand. I was drawn to a light in her and I wanted to know what it was. She was the one held captive and yet, being in the room with her, it felt like I was the one who was bound." Tears tightened her throat. "I interrogated her for days."

"Did Julian know?"

"No. Normally he'd be the first to know anything, but I didn't tell anyone."

"You hurt her?"

"A little, yeah. She was so brave. But I didn't know why I couldn't do more. Every day I visited her, I promised myself it would be the last. But every day I kept asking her more questions. I lied to myself that I wanted to know who she was working for. But what I really wanted to know was why."

"Why what?"

"I don't know. Why everything. Why was she like she was. Why did I feel the way I did…But God held her tongue until the time was right and I was ready to hear. Then she showed me how to find the treasure I was searching for but couldn't name."

"Is that when you escaped with her?"

"No. I continued to work for Julian for a while."

"What about the night you fell in the river?"

"That was after he knew I'd turned on him. I tried to break into his house, but they were waiting for me. It was a miracle I even got away. I trained with all Julian's guys. They knew my strengths and weaknesses as much as I knew theirs. In the end I think it was Tyler who got me. He's always been good at thinking ahead. I don't know why I went into the open at the side of the river. It was a stupid move. I should have known one of them would catch up to me there."

"Or you were where God wanted you to be. It's what saved you in the end."

"I suppose that's true."

"But why go back to Julian's house in the first place?"

"Growing up, whenever I got out of line, Julian would threaten me that if I ever left him, he'd easily find another to replace me."

"You think he meant it?"

"I knew he meant it. I knew he was training up other kids. He'd been doing it for years. He raised people up and put them in influential positions that he could control. He would often rave about some new child he'd identified. He was proud of them and it made me jealous. It made me want to please him more, which I guess was the point."

"You must have caused him some trouble for him to manipulate you like that."

"I was strongheaded but no, I adored Julian. He had no need to threaten me in that way. I never would have left him. Or at least, I never thought I would. For a long time, I worshiped him. I was so proud to be his daughter when the rest of the kids were only his students. When I finally did leave him, I almost turned back. In fact, if it weren't for Lynn, I probably would have."

"Even after you found Jesus, he still had a hold on you?"

"Not like that. I didn't want him to do to another what he'd done to me. When I went to his house that night, it was to see who had taken my place and to try to rescue them if I could."

"Was anyone there?"

"I should have realized it was a setup. A leaked news report praised Julian for adopting a girl who had lost her parents. It may have been true, but he knows me too well. He knew I'd come back. They were watching and waiting."

"I heard him talking when they had me in the basement. Julian must have thought I was unconscious when he was speaking about it, but he does have a girl. I think her name is Katy. It sounded like she was new."

"Katy."

"Yeah. I think so. But even if you'd rescued one child, he'd find another."

"Then I'd save that one and then the next and the next. You said yourself we needed to move one step at a time. Each child is a step."

"Then we have to find a way to stop him for good. And once this is over, we're going to revisit this idea of you running away from the only people in your life who care about you."

Chapter 17

JULIAN DUCKED his head under the beam when he reached the bottom of the stairs.

He could hear voices across the room but couldn't see them through the maze of crates.

Good. It was important they understood he could turn up at any time without giving them notice.

He wove his way around the boxes but stopped before reaching the back of the room where he knew Tyler was with another of his men.

"So Chicago and DC are the only two?" Tyler said.

"So far," the other man said. It sounded like Clarkson.

"You're expecting more?"

"We're trying to be prepared, sir."

"What you should be prepared for is success. We're already on a tight schedule."

Julian cleared his throat as he stepped into the open space. "I quite agree with you, Tyler. I'd prefer your comments remained positive in nature, Clarkson. Unless you know of a specific problem. Then I expect a proper solution."

"Yes, sir," Clarkson said as both men stood at attention.

"Julian, we weren't expecting you to come down today," Tyler said.

"Am I not allowed to check on the progress of my own plans?"

"You know that's not what I mean." Tyler rested a hand on top of a crate. "I'd rather you didn't spend too much time in a room full of explosives. We can't afford to have anything happen to you."

"I'm more concerned that the room is still so full of explosives than I am about them exploding while I'm down here. The last time we discussed our progress, you assured me we were on schedule."

"We still are. There have been some delays for various reasons, but most will be out before the end of the week."

"These delays, do they have anything to do with Chicago and DC?"

"That is part of it, yes."

"You didn't think it was worth informing me of any problems?"

"Not when it's unnecessary. You have us on your team because we get the job done. I'm getting it sorted. You have more important issues to deal with at the moment. And to be honest, sir, with a coordinated attack this large, we expected more problems than we've encountered. To date, we have had no issues with any of the individuals in charge of the smaller scale assaults."

Julian smiled. "Well stated. I do expect the plans to be a success. It's written in the stars." When Tyler gave him an odd look, Julian added, "So to speak." Tyler was already spooked. He didn't need to add to the man's unease, not when he was so close to his goal.

"Of course."

"What I would like to know is what happened in Chicago and DC."

"As I said, we've got it under control."

"Then why are you avoiding telling me?"

Tyler's lips puckered as he held back a sigh. "One of the guys in Chicago used the warehouse we were housing him in to cook meth. The police got wind of it and got a warrant."

"And?"

"And the warehouse was raided."

"Was the literature in place by then?"

"That was the first thing we established with all the outposts."

"So it's not a total loss, then?"

"No. But Chicago will be postponed until we can set up another team out there."

"And DC?"

"Teddy had a crisis of conscience."

"Teddy?"

"Yes."

Julian's jaw worked as he got himself back under control. "He was one of our best. That's why we put him in DC in the first place."

"I know. But he said he couldn't do it anymore. He didn't explain why."

"I take it you asked properly?"

"Yes, sir."

"And he didn't give you anything?"

"Nothing. But I do believe Eva had a connection in DC. Maybe it's related."

"Have you already taken care of Teddy?"

"We have."

"That's an unfortunate loss. But there's nothing more we can do besides get someone else ready to take his position. Someone who can't be persuaded by their conscience."

"Did you have someone in mind?"

"I'll think about it and let you know. But I believe it will be for the best in the end. Is everyone else ready?"

"We've reshuffled the chain of attacks. Everyone will be in place and ready once you give us word to execute the plan."

"Perfect." He clapped Tyler on the shoulder. "You've done an excellent job. Both of you. When the dust settles, we will be ready to finally see everything come together. It will be magnificent."

***

Clara shuffled toward Eva and Ben, keeping her eyes focused on Ben. "How is everyone this mornin'?"

"It's okay," Eva said. "I'm not going to hurt you."

Clara's eyes flashed with fire and she pushed her shoulders back. "You think that's what I'm worried about? You hurtin' me? I'm more afraid I'll break ya."

"Oh...Well, you won't. I'm not made of glass."

Clara looked down into her basket of eggs. "I guess you won't be eating eggs anymore."

"Why not?"

"You said you didn't used to like 'em."

Eva took an egg from the basket. "I may have gotten my memory back, but that doesn't mean I've lost anything of myself. Yesterday I liked eggs, and I've decided that today I like eggs."

A smile lit up Clara's face, but she hid it quickly behind a scowl. "Guess I'll have to go get cookin' then. You two better not lose track of time. Otherwise your eggs will get rubbery and you best not go blamin' me for it."

"Yes, ma'am," Ben said. "We're right behind you." He hurried after Clara, but when Eva didn't follow, he stopped.

"What's wrong?"

She walked slowly toward him. "Katy."

"I'm sorry I mentioned her."

"Why?"

"Because I should have known it would upset you."

"Shouldn't it upset me? Julian's got another little girl right now that he's...She doesn't deserve it. I can't let him do that again. We have to stop him."

"And we will. We've got the list and now that you have your memory back, you'll know what to do with it when you're ready."

"How does that help Katy?"

"Stopping Julian will help Katy."

"No. I can't let him have her."

"Eva. I don't know what you think you can do, but whatever it is, it's too dangerous."

"Then help me."

"No. I don't feel right about this."

"Fine then, stay here. I'll be back once the girl is safe."

"Morning," Lynn said from the door.

"Lynn. Good," Ben said. "Maybe you can talk some sense into her."

"Oh, I don't know about that. What's going on?"

Eva stalked into the house. "Ben's upset because I want to go save Katy."

"Who's Katy?"

"The girl Julian got to replace me."

"Where is she?"

"She'll be at Julian's house."

"What's this now?" Clara said. "Did you say you're going back to Julian's house? No way. I object."

"I can't move forward until I know she's safe."

"Eva." Ben grabbed her arm and turned her toward him. "You're letting your emotions cloud your judgment."

"So what if I am? I've spent the last twenty years devoid of emotion."

"That's not true."

"It is."

"You don't—"

"No. Stop. I already know what you're going to say. But you can't convince me otherwise. Even before I lost my memory, my past has been like a giant wave that keeps knocking me under every time I try to stand. I can't ever get my feet under me, so I do my best to keep my head above water. That's all I can do."

"I'm sorry this is so hard for you. I'm sorry for all the things Julian did to you. But you were only a kid."

"Yeah, but I was his kid."

"So what?"

"You don't understand."

"Then help me to."

"Julian chose kids who showed, even at a young age, that they could turn everything off. He specifically chooses children who have no conscience, and he always said to me that he was blessed with a child who was the best of the best. That's why I have to save Katy. He will nurture the darkness inside of her until it consumes her."

"But Jesus saved you. He can save Katy. You can't go rushing into a situation like that just because you feel bad."

"Then what do you propose I do?"

Ben huffed. "We should pray."

Eva's face blanked. She should have known that would be his response. "You're trying to stall me."

"Is that what you really think?"

"Fine. We'll pray. But I won't change my mind." She walked to the door. "I'll do my praying outside."

As she stomped across the lawn, her frustration grew. She knew that having God with them was their only way forward, but she had never been one to ask permission. She often had conversations with God as she went, but found that her instincts were a good guide, and she trusted that God knew her well enough to lead her that way.

Her thoughts drifted to Julian, bringing with them an uncomfortable pang. She'd told Ben about his threats, but she hadn't been completely honest. The concern she had for Katy's safety was only part of it. But her drive to rescue the girl was tied to jealousy. How could Julian find it so easy to replace her? It was stupid and horrible, but maybe if she looked into the eyes of this innocent child, maybe it would be enough to help Eva finally be completely free of him.

She hurried back to the house. "I've prayed about it. I'm going."

Clara had been mumbling prayers into her lap. "Are you sure?" she said when she looked up.

"Yes. We need to rescue her."

Lynn was leaning against the wall, biting her lip. "Eva." She looked at the other two in the room. "I don't think that's what the rest of us are feeling."

"I'm with Lynn," Ben said. "I don't think you can trust yourself right now."

Eva ground her teeth. "You said to pray and I prayed. Now, I don't expect any of you to come with me, but you're not going to stop me."

"Please, wait." Ben stood and reached for her, but she moved away. "We can't support you in this."

"Fine. I'll see you back here with the girl."

"Eva."

But she was out the door.

Ben threw his arms up in the air and turned to Clara. "She is impossible. I liked her better when she had no memory."

"I'll second that. Although…I like her spunk."

"It would be endearing if it weren't so infuriating. She's going to get herself killed for real this time."

"But it's her own life that's in danger. Not yours."

"That doesn't bother you?"

"Of course it bothers me." Clara sighed. "You wouldn't understand."

"Understand what?"

"It doesn't matter. You're not a mother."

"What does that have to do with anything?"

"You really think any of us could have done anything to stop her walking out that door? You think there was something—anything you could say to change her mind?"

"Maybe not." He looked outside when he heard the truck drive off. "I should have gone with her."

"Why didn't you?"

"I don't know. Stubbornness?"

"Or wisdom," Lynn said.

Ben shook his head. "I find it hard to tell the difference when it comes to Eva."

"You like her," Clara said.

Ben looked startled. "What is it with you two? I just don't want anyone to get hurt."

"But you like her." Clara pushed.

"I like you too."

She burst out laughing. "If you looked at me the way you look at her, I'd be worried. I'm glad you've warmed to me, but we both know that's not what I'm talkin' 'bout."

"There's nothing going on between me and Eva. I've already had this conversation with Lynn."

"But your feelings for her cloud your judgment just like her emotions are clouding hers."

"For argument's sake, let's say that's true, not that I'm admitting to anything. But then, what do we do?"

"Same thing we've been doin'. Or are you a quitter?"

"Clara's right." Lynn sat at the table. "It doesn't feel like we have time, but we have to pray...again."

Chapter 18

EVA ALREADY KNEW what to do when she got close to Julian's house. It was close to dusk and she had her plan ready. The same as last time. The only reason it hadn't worked last time was because Julian knew she was coming. He wouldn't know tonight.

She made her way to the park and the small door hidden among the bushes where she and Ben had escaped before. She knew the butler's movements this time of the night, as well as how to remain undetected from any other prying eyes that might be watching.

When she had no memory, Julian had told her part of the house was closed for renovations. She knew now that was a lie, and that meant she knew where he was keeping Katy.

Staying close to the hedge, she moved along the edge of the property until she could get a look inside through a large bay window.

Light filtered onto the lawn past a curtain that was almost fully drawn. From her position, she could see one area of the room where she identified Bea sitting on a couch talking with a young girl who looked to be about eight or nine. The girl laughed at something Bea had said, then stood and went to the window and looked out.

Eva dropped to the ground and wriggled into the bush where the branches scraped at her. Katy couldn't have seen Eva in the dark, but the directness of the girl's gaze made her feel like she had a spotlight pointed at her.

The girl looked back at Bea and shook her head, then moved into a part of the room where Eva couldn't see her.

Eva checked the time when Bea ushered the girl out of the room. It was nine. The bedtime Julian had always set for her growing up. He didn't choose things like bedtime arbitrarily. Everything had a purpose, so Eva kept watch for the next light that would go on and give her the position of Katy's room.

It wasn't long before a room on the second floor lit up and then another few minutes before the lights went back out. She'd give time for things to settle before climbing up to the room where she would try to convince Katy to come away with a stranger in the night. No small feat.

Dark thoughts pried their way into Eva's mind as every shadow curled into a grotesque memory of the horrors she'd done.

She blinked them away and tried to focus on banal thoughts to keep her mind clear, but it remained clouded.

Yanking off her glove, she ran her fingers through

the grass, feeling for a thick blade suitable for eliciting that terrible honking noise Ben had shown her. After sliding a suitable piece between her thumbs, she pressed the instrument to her mouth, but had no intention of blowing.

The damp grass against her lips settled her thoughts but made her miss Ben's presence. If he had come with her, she would have been more settled. He had a way of stilling the edginess that threatened to break her focus. And as she sat alone in the eerie silence, she began to battle with her decision to come, a feeling she quickly pushed aside. She was committed to this and wouldn't leave without Katy. She couldn't abandon her now. Not when she was so close.

Her fingers ran the length of the grass repeatedly as she wondered what the others were doing. She could see the look Ben gave her when she refused to give in. Then she remembered the way he'd looked at her when he sat on the step.

With a silent grunt, she flicked the grass away, breaking the distraction. It wasn't the diversion she needed and she couldn't sit still any longer. It was time to set her plan in motion.

Silently, she climbed the side of the house and leaped onto the balcony, where she tucked herself into the corner next to a potted plant and listened before slipping into place next to the door.

She picked the lock and paused with her hand on the slim handle, focusing on her breathing. Katy was about to meet a stranger who would ask her to leave her home in the middle of the night. But Eva knew what it was to be Julian's favorite and she was probably the only one who knew what to say to gain Katy's cooperation and trust.

She pushed a thin stream of breath between her lips before pulling down on the handle and opening the door. When she stepped inside, a breeze followed her in, ruffling the drapes that hung from a large four-poster bed. But she nearly retreated when she saw the girl sitting on the edge of the bed with her legs dangling, watching her.

Eva held her breath before taking another step into the room, holding her hands out to show they were empty.

"Katy, I'm not here to hurt you. Julian sent me."

"I know who you are." The girl's voice was lilting as though they were playing a game.

"You do?"

"Yup. He told me you were coming."

Eva's throat closed over her next breath. It took her a moment before she could respond. "Julian told you I was coming?"

"No. Harold."

She couldn't decide whether to advance or retreat. The instincts she relied on were failing her. She felt the danger but couldn't decipher if it was fear or a warning.

Making a decision, she took a step forward. "Harold, huh?" She couldn't remember anyone named Harold. "I didn't know you knew him."

"He's my friend."

"Really? He's a friend of mine too."

"No he's not. You're lying."

Her feet ached to flee, but she wouldn't let them. "You're a smart girl. I can see why Julian thinks so highly of you. But you're right, I don't know Harold. Does he work for Julian?"

Katy giggled. "That's funny. Harold didn't tell me you were funny."

"I'm not usually. Is Harold nearby? Maybe I should meet him." Her hand went slowly to her back, where she had a gun.

"You can't. Harold only shows himself to those who are worthy. You're not worthy. He told me."

"He did, did he?"

"Yes."

Eva licked her lips. "I guess whatever Harold says goes?"

"He's very smart—I wouldn't do that if I were you."

"Do what?"

"Harold says you should keep your hands where I can see them."

Eva held out her empty hands in front of her again. "I don't have anything."

"You shouldn't have come."

"Why not? Julian asked me to, and you know we do what Julian wants. Did he forget to tell you I would be here tonight? He's created a special test. Just for you. Not for anyone else." Eva had always loved it when Julian had things made for her only.

Katy slipped off the bed and walked forward, but stopped a few feet away.

Eva let out a shaky breath. It was going to work.

"I know about the test," Katy said, clasping her hands behind her back. "But it's not Julian's, it's Harold's."

"Okay, sure. Julian didn't tell me it was Harold's idea, but either way, it doesn't matter."

Katy giggled again. "It matters very much."

"Okay. Then let's do Harold's idea."

"You say that like it's your choice." The room was illuminated by the moon enough that Eva could see the gleam of white teeth when the girl smiled. It sent a shiver up her spine.

Katy took a step closer and tipped her head to the side. "You're smaller than I expected."

Eva's stomach churned, and she took a step back, but it was too late. Katy sprang for her, clinging and scraping her fingernails across Eva's face.

Eva swallowed the scream that threatened to alert the house of her presence. She tried to pry Katy off her, but the girl was strong and the reality of what she'd walked into had her mind screaming to heaven for help.

Katy let out a shrill cry, and Eva's muscles tightened. She jerked the girl away and somehow threw her off. Without taking the time to process the situation further, Eva raced onto the balcony, yanking the door closed behind her. She couldn't remember climbing down to the ground, but suddenly found herself kneeling in the wet grass.

Katy let out a gargling scream that sent Eva sprinting across the lawn to the bushes, where she dove toward her escape. But as she scrambled to get through the small door, someone grabbed her ankle. She kicked back hard, dislodging the grip and pulling herself the rest of the way through.

She pulled her gun as she darted across the park. The woods near the river she'd tried to escape in last time were close.

But after reaching the trees, she slipped into what felt like a nightmare. She could remember the same grip of fear as she dodged branches to escape. She surrendered to her instincts as a dark pit filled her stomach. If they got her this time, she wouldn't escape with her life again.

Her lungs burned and she pushed herself harder than before. Branches caught her clothes, tearing at her skin, but she didn't slow down. When her shirt caught on a limb, the gun slipped from her hand. She grunted but didn't stop to retrieve it. Ripping free of the tree, she pushed her feet hard into the dirt to pick up speed.

The memory of Katy jumping at her blinded her for a moment as she got caught by another branch. She pushed the image away, but tears restricted her vision and her muscles were heavy with fear.

She tripped and nearly fell, but caught herself and swung around a tree trunk. But before she could reset her course, something shoved her sideways and a weight landed on her, pushing her down into the dirt. Her elbow struck a rock, sending a searing pain up her arm. She struggled, driving her knee into her attacker, but he blocked it and wrestled her down, pinning her so she couldn't move.

He covered her mouth with his hand. "Don't move," he hissed into her ear.

A scream stuck in her throat as terror threatened to consume her.

Chapter 19

IN DESPERATION EVA threw her shoulder up and caught her opponent somewhere in the face. He grunted but didn't loosen his grip on her.

"Eva, stop. Stop moving. It's me. Lie still."

Ben's voice dragged a bleat from her throat but then she quieted. Tears dripped onto the ground as relief took the place of fear.

His face was close to hers and she angled her head so her forehead pressed into his chin. "Ben."

"Shh."

She struggled to steady her ragged breathing but with Ben's weight on top of her, it was hard to suck in the oxygen she needed.

Swallowing back the thickness in her mouth, she attempted to slow her breathing. She had the training to deal with this. With her whole focus on each breath, the rest of the world faded for a moment while she quieted her breathing and her heart rate slowed.

Running steps came close and Ben's head curled

down so his breath was hot against her cheek. His arms tightened around her, and they both held their breath as the sound of boots stomping through the woods came within feet.

Someone yelled from another part of the woods, "This way! She's gone toward the river."

The sound of the man near them retreated and Eva whimpered into the dirt but quickly steadied herself as Ben lifted her off the ground. He pushed the hair off her face and leaned in close, looking into her eyes to get her to focus on him. "I didn't hurt you too bad, did I? Can you still run?"

She nodded and he squeezed her hand, pulling her in a direction opposite the way the man had run.

"That was lucky," Eva said once they'd cleared the woods.

"Not luck." His voice was cold.

"Why'd they go to the river? Did your friend Felix help you again?"

"Didn't need him. Clara makes plenty of noise."

Eva yanked Ben to a stop. "Clara's out there? What if they find her?"

"She'll be fine. Trust me. We need to get you out of here."

"But how—"

"We can talk about that later. Let's go." His tone spoke louder than his words and the shame that flushed her cheeks made the scratches on her face burn.

"How'd you get here?"

"We borrowed Lynn's car."

"Wait, she's here too?"

"No. She's back at Clara's. Let's go. We have to keep moving."

He walked her out of the clearing to where she'd parked the truck. "How'd you know where I parked?"

"It's the same place I would have. Keys?" He held out his hand and waited until she handed them over.

———

Ben drove about a mile down the road and pulled onto a side street, where he stopped.

"Why are we stopping?" Eva said.

"Clara. She's meeting us here."

"You said she'd be okay?"

"She will be."

Eva leaned her head back onto the seat. "I messed up."

"Yup."

"You have every right to be mad at me. I shouldn't even be allowed to participate anymore. How can you trust me again?"

Ben sighed. "No one expects you to get it right all the time."

"That's all you have to say about it?"

"You want me to scold you? You're a grown woman."

"But I put everyone at risk."

"You put yourself at risk. Clara and I decided for ourselves. Besides, I don't need to be hard on you. You're doing enough of that yourself. Trust me, I know the drill."

"I'm so sorry."

"You had been through a traumatic event, getting your memory back. I'm not surprised you did what you did. You were confused. You did what you thought was right at the time."

Her head dropped. "That's not entirely true."

"What do you mean?"

Eva bit her lip to keep it from trembling. "I can't escape him."

"Who, Julian?"

"I tried to convince myself that I wanted to help that girl."

"You didn't?"

"I did, but the truth is so much worse."

Ben gripped the wheel. "You were jealous of her?"

"How do you know that?"

"It makes sense."

"It doesn't make you sick? Because it makes me sick to think that Julian still has a grip on me like that. I thought if I saved Katy, then I could prove something to myself and be free of him, but I can't. All I've done is let you all down, and I'm still controlled by a psychopath."

"It's not sick. And it doesn't prove he still has a hold on you."

"Yes, it does. It might seem impossible, but I know how I feel."

Ben blew out a breath. "When I was in high school, I dated this girl. I really liked her, and I thought she felt the same."

"Are you trying to make me jealous of you now?"

He laughed. "Maybe if I thought it would work. But

no, I saw her with another guy. I found out she wasn't the girl I thought she was, and I wondered what I liked about her in the first place."

"That is nothing like this."

"Let me finish. The strange thing was that for the next several months, I found myself showing off whenever she was around. I wanted her to want me back— not because I was interested in her, not because I wanted to date her again, but because I didn't like being rejected. Julian's hold on you is because of his rejection, not because you actually still want to be with him."

That made sense, but she was afraid to believe it. Afraid it wasn't true for her. "What'd you do to get over her?"

"I forgave her."

Eva closed her eyes. "I don't want to forgive Julian. Not ever."

"I know. But you're going to have to someday."

"And if I can't?"

"Then he'll always have a place inside you. And I think you'd rather forgive him than give him that."

"That doesn't change the fact that I screwed up."

"Fine. Yes. You screwed up. But you're going to have to get over it because we've got work to do. You're a valuable part of this team and not just because you have inside knowledge."

"Stop being nice to me."

"I'm telling you the truth. You have a lot to offer. But you do need to slow down and stop reacting. Promise me you've learned your lesson."

"I have. I promise."

"Good."

She stared out into the darkness while they waited. "How did you know where to find me? How'd you know I'd be escaping through the woods?"

"We didn't. We asked God for wisdom and came up with a plan."

"Oh."

"Hey, can I ask you something?"

"Of course."

"Why did he choose Katy?"

"He would have seen something in her."

"But, I mean, usually with men like Julian, they want an heir to take over from them when they die. I'm surprised he didn't choose a boy."

"Oh that? No. It's his father who'd go on and on about the bloodline. How men are meant to dominate. Julian's different. He wanted to be the last man. He wanted to make sure that no other man came after him to take more credit."

"He wants to leave a legacy of one. I wonder what he would have done if you were a boy." Ben pinched his lip. "He didn't want you to go on to do greater things?"

"He did. But even if I was great, he'd still be the last man."

"Interesting."

"But...there was something really strange about Katy."

"You saw her?"

"Yeah. I got into her bedroom and I thought I was close to getting her out of there, but...I don't know. Something was wrong."

"What happened?"

"She attacked me and screamed. That's how the guards were alerted."

"You expected her to react differently?"

"No. I know Julian's been training her to fight, but that's not what happened. You know how Felix helped us escape, and you were talking about seeing demons and stuff? And when we were driving into town to get Lynn, you prayed that they wouldn't see us and know what we were doing."

"Yeah."

"I think you're right."

"You saw something?"

"Kind of. Have you ever seen someone possessed?"

"Not that I know of. Why?"

"This is going to sound crazy."

"I doubt it."

"These scratches on my face didn't come from running in the woods. Katy did it."

"When she attacked you."

"Yeah."

"That doesn't mean she was possessed."

"That's not what I mean. She was sitting up in her bed when I went in the room and she said Harold told her I was coming."

"Who's Harold?"

"I didn't know at first, but after what happened…the only Harold I've ever heard of was my—Julian's great-great-grandfather."

"You think she's talking to a dead man?"

"Or a demon. I don't know. I don't know how this

stuff works, but when she jumped on me, she was still several feet away. And she was super strong. I almost couldn't get her off. If I hadn't prayed...It just wasn't natural."

"That makes sense."

"You believe me?"

"Over the last couple of weeks, even before we met, I've felt the darkness growing. Felix has mentioned things that make me think there's a war going on that we can't see, and whatever the devil has planned, we're getting in his way. I never knew Julian was into that kind of stuff, but he must be exposing her to it. Were you ever exposed to it?"

Eva shook her head. "This was never what it was like when I was there. We were trained to read people and control them, but 'Harold' never turned up. Julian was always adamant about serving no one. He never believed in a higher power besides himself. And even then, it wasn't in a spiritual sense."

"Then where did it come from?"

"It must be Bea."

"Bea?"

"Mrs. Beaman. She's sort of like a nanny. She helps with the training, and she always did these meditation things with me. I remember there was this one time that she tried to hypnotize me and she couldn't do it. She was so angry she slapped me across the face. It was the only time I saw Julian truly angry at her."

"But what do you mean, she couldn't do it?"

"I wouldn't go under. I didn't really want to. I didn't like the idea of her having control over me in an unconscious state. Bea was always kind to me, but I never felt comfortable with her."

"So, you think she's responsible?"

"I don't know who else it could be. And if Katy knew I was coming because she's got a spirit speaking to her, then we can't go against Julian without our own spiritual—" The door of the truck scraped open and Eva jumped.

Clara climbed in, laughing. "That's the most fun I've had in years. I had those boys so turned around, they wouldn't know their own hand in front of their face. You should have seen them. Big boys too. They were mad. I don't know what you did, Eva, but they were intent on tearing you to shreds."

"They didn't hurt you?" Eva said.

"An ugly old lady like me? No way." She clapped her hands together. "What's next?"

Eva looked at Ben. "I'll do whatever you guys say. Whatever you think is right is what we'll do."

"That's not acceptable," he said. "I want your input. We'll go back to the house and regroup. We have that list to look at still."

"And I've already wasted more time," Eva grumbled.

"All the more reason we need you to be a vocal part of our next step. Clara, you follow us back in Lynn's car."

Clara patted Eva on the shoulder. "Don't worry about it, honey. We can all be a bunch of boneheaded clodpolls together."

Chapter 20

"EVA!" Lynn ran from the house. She pulled her friend into a tight hug when she got out of the truck. "I was praying so hard." When she pulled back, she put a hand on Eva's face. "What happened?"

"Let's just say your prayers were very important. There's more going on than we realized. Let's get cleaned up and we can have a look at that list."

"No," Ben said. "We're going to get cleaned up and get a few hours of sleep. There's nothing more we can do tonight."

"But I've already wasted so much time."

"A few more hours isn't going to matter."

"I'm with Ben," Clara said. "We can start again at sunup."

"All right," Eva said. "We'll get a couple of hours, but I want to get started as soon as there's light in the sky."

Ben was already up reading a Bible when Eva got up. "You sent us all to bed and didn't get any sleep yourself?" Eva scolded.

"I slept. Don't worry."

She sat down at the table with the list of names and sighed as she ran her hand across the crinkled page.

"Is something wrong?" Ben asked.

"I thought I had remembered everything."

"Something else came back?"

"Not a lost memory so much as the reality of the people on this list."

"There are people on there you had forgotten about?"

"There are people on this list I've never met. But there are a lot I know."

"And?"

She looked up at Ben. "I helped Julian with this. I helped him turn people."

"And that's why you can help turn them back. Help them to understand the horrible plan they are a part of. They need to understand how evil the Underwood Foundation really is."

"You two didn't start the party without me, did ya?" Clara said with a sniff when she entered the room.

"Wouldn't dream of it," Ben said. "Should we get Lynn up?"

"She's up. She'll be out in a minute."

They sat quietly together until everyone was assembled at the table.

Eva cleared her throat. "If everyone is happy to put

last night behind us for now, I should probably start by explaining the problem with the bill."

"I'd say we're all on board with that," Clara said.

Eva looked at the other two, who nodded. "Okay. Julian has always wanted one thing. Control. If that bill gets passed, then when it comes into effect, he'll be ready to access any information, phones, computers, video, satellites. Everything."

"We've worked out that much," Ben said. "But how would he access it? And how would he keep it once the threat is gone? I don't see the danger there."

"That, my friend," Clara said, "is how conspiracies come to pass."

"What does that have to do with conspiracies?"

"The bill will be approved because no one thinks there is a threat to their safety. They sleep well knowing that if everything goes wrong, the government will fix it. But until that time—which in their minds is never—they are safe. It's an impossible scenario. That's why it will work."

"But that would mean Julian expects something to happen."

"He doesn't need to expect something to happen. He can make it happen, can't he?"

Ben shook his head. "That would take a very difficult, very coordinated attack."

Eva rested her head in her hands. "That's what's so overwhelming about it. He's been preparing for this for years. This isn't a plan he's made up recently. Ben, when you blew up that building, it set Julian back, but that facility and what he used it for was not his ultimate goal. It was only one step. This all started with—"

"What is it?"

"Harold. This all started with Harold. Julian picked up where he left off." She pressed her hand to her mouth. "Does that mean…" She couldn't say it.

"So this *is* bigger than we thought," Ben said. "Okay, so Julian picked up where Harold left off and continued putting the right people in the right places for this moment in history."

"Yes. They're his army, but—"

"We can't worry about the larger nature of what's going on. We need to focus on what we can do with the bill for now and trust that God's got the rest under control."

"Okay. You're right."

"And I'm still not seeing how it's possible. Even if Julian has supernatural help, I don't understand how he can pull it off."

Clara blew out a raspberry. "Sounds to me like you're trying to sweep this all away." Her back stiffened, and she leaned in toward Ben. "Where did you say you came from? How do we know you're not a plant?"

"Clara," Eva said.

Clara laughed. "Can't I have a little fun? We're all so uptight, and watching him squirm relaxes me."

Ben sighed. "I don't mean to play the devil's advocate here. But even if he could orchestrate the look of a terrorist attack on American soil, how does he intend to get access to all that information and then keep getting access to it once the threat is gone?"

"That's what I've been telling you. He's got the right people in the right places. He's been working in the background to make sure that the Underwood Foundation wins the bid as the organization that gathers the information. He's probably building it right now."

"Where?"

"I don't know. But if this bill passes, then Julian will have the backing of the US government to create whatever he needs to gain access to everything. He already has most of the technology he needs. And when the threat is gone and they order him to turn off the switch, he won't."

Ben ran his hands through his hair. "Okay, that fills in a few pieces, but you talked about a final goal with all of this. I know you said he wants control, but how far does that go?"

"For his lukewarm followers, he's always said it's about making a utopian society, but for those of us on the inside, it was always about being the most powerful man, not just in the United States, but the whole world. He already has some very influential people around the world in his pockets. If he can control one country, he'll work at taking the next."

Clara jumped up, slamming her hands onto the table. "One world order." Her puffy face was wide-eyed. "He's the antichrist. I knew it. I could feel it in my bones."

"You're getting ahead of yourself," Ben said. "I'm not sure we're there yet."

"How can you say that? It's coming, you know. Julian is positioning himself. It's coming."

"Before we give Julian the distinguished honor of being the cornerstone for end times, I'd like to know what will happen if we can stop the bill." He looked at Eva.

"He won't give up on his dream while he has breath, but it would certainly delay his plans. And it's what we were trying to do before I lost my memory."

"Wonderful, so that brings us to your plan. If you're ready."

"There's no more time to waste. Ready or not. We've got to move forward on this."

"But you still think it will work?" Lynn said.

"I think so. Originally, I wanted to turn as many people away from Julian as we could because I wanted to make right what I'd already done, but I'll have to worry about that later. Right now, we have to focus on simply making sure the bill is not approved. This list has all the names we need. And now I know what to do with it."

"Tell me who I need to speak to and I'll head back to DC right away."

"Okay, I went back through the names this morning and I've crossed off anyone we need to steer clear of." She slid the paper closer to Lynn. "If any of these people find out what you're up to, you're done. You have to promise me you'll be as safe as you can."

"You know I will."

"Start with the blue highlighted names first. If they know the truth about what's going on, they should be easy to turn and they'll be able to help reach others. After that, move on to the yellow, then the green."

Lynn ran her finger down the row of names. "Any of these blue names where you'd suggest I start?"

"Do you know Sarah Hostetter?"

"We've had coffee a couple of times. I'm glad to see her name is blue although I'm disappointed she's on here at all. Wait—Mark Claven? His name's crossed off."

"Yeah."

"Julian has something on him?"

"No, Mark's one of Julian's early recruits. Why?"

Lynn shook her head. "Nothing to worry about. He's a friend. Or I thought he was."

"You haven't told him anything?"

"No."

"Good. Steer clear of him from now on."

Lynn nodded, but she looked sad. "I'll call Sarah on my way back and get an early appointment."

"Julian barely had her onside. She may have already changed her mind, but she follows the crowd because it's the crowd. Julian thinks she's an easy shoo-in, but I've watched her. I was never convinced she was an absolute. If you explain how dangerous the bill is, I think she'll turn. Other than that, you work with your group and do the best you can."

"Okay. I'll let you know once I have her response. And what about you guys? What's your next move?"

Eva pointed at a name at the bottom of the list. "I'm going to see Congressman Lyons."

Lynn balked. "Are you sure? You've crossed him out. Even *I* can understand why."

"Ooh," Clara said. "I've heard of him. What's in his

closet? Does he have a secret second family in another country?"

"Clara, please," Ben said.

"It's an honest question."

"He's close friends with Julian," Eva said. "He stands for most of what Julian does."

"Hang on." Ben put a hand up. "Are you sure about this?"

"You have every right not to trust me."

"It's not that, but you said we're only going after people we have a chance of turning. You think you'll turn this guy Lyons?"

"He's become…unsure. I saw it in him. I almost alerted Julian to it."

"Why didn't you?"

Eva looked at the table in thought. "I don't know. Maybe because by then, I was unsure. Lyons is a good man. I've known him most of my life. And while he's always supported Julian, it's mostly been on a peer level. He agrees with the society Julian says he wants to create, but he's always been uncomfortable with the lines Julian crosses. I think if Lyons had a reason to go against him, he would. We just have to be convincing."

Ben squeezed his forehead. "We can't risk going to a friend of Julian's."

"We have—No. I'm sorry. You're right. If you don't feel right about it, we'll go another way."

"Can you just explain to me why he's worth the risk?"

"He's always been the linchpin. If we can shift him, a whole lot more will follow. Because we're short on time, it's an easy way to get a lot of people across the line...and I care about him. He's always been kind to me."

"It would be a huge win for us," Lynn said. "But if you don't turn him, he could alert Julian."

"We'll pray about it," Ben said.

Eva's shoulders dropped. "You want to pray."

"I know it's not what you want to hear."

"No. Don't misunderstand. I didn't think you'd even consider Lyons. Okay. We'll pray. Lynn, you get back to DC and we'll be in touch."

"This will work," Lynn said as she got up to go. "God wouldn't have brought us all together for nothing."

Clara rubbed a hand across her mouth after Lynn disappeared down the driveway. "I appreciate Lynn's enthusiasm, but is anyone else anxious that things could go either way right now?"

"Sometimes that's the price of faith," Eva said, feeling a twinge at the loss of Lynn's steadying presence.

Chapter 21

EVERYONE AGREED to spend time in prayer before settling on Lyons, but Eva had trouble focusing on the plan. Images of Katy smiling at her in the dark kept distracting her. Facing down a grown man trained in combat was one thing, but she wasn't prepared for a little girl. She understood tactics of manipulation and distraction and how to discover weaknesses to use them to gain control, but this enemy was different.

It shouldn't surprise her that Julian had allowed Bea's ideology to infiltrate his training. He used the weakest and most vulnerable members of society to build his power base, no matter the cost. This was simply another tactic. But whenever she thought of Katy and the way the girl had looked at her and spoken to her, it sickened her in a way she couldn't have imagined. She knew they needed God to fight the enemy, but she couldn't get her head around what was happening beyond the natural.

"How're you doing?" Clara said, poking her head into the bedroom where Eva had retreated to.

"Shouldn't you be praying?"

"I have. I know my stance on things, but I can't help feeling like you're struggling a little."

"I'm having trouble processing last night."

"Ah, speaking of last night…" Clara disappeared for a minute, then came back with a small flat jar. She sat next to Eva on the bed. "Look at me."

"What's that?"

Clara dipped her pinkie into the jar and rubbed the contents onto the scratches on Eva's face. "I meant to do this earlier, but got distracted. Don't want that getting infected."

Eva scrunched up her nose. "What's in that? It smells terrible."

"Sorry about the smell. The best stuff usually stinks the worst." She tucked the jar into her pocket, then stretched, letting out a deep groan as she twisted from one side to the other. "Now. About last night. You're rattled."

"I am."

"Not surprised, considering what you saw. You scared?"

"A little."

"Well, don't be. The scariest ones are the easiest to defeat."

"I don't know. There was a moment when I wasn't sure I could."

"Did you cry out to God?"

"In a manner of speaking. It wasn't eloquent."

"You think God wants you to be eloquent?"

"I'm just glad he knows what I mean when I can't get the words out right. I was completely freaked out and that doesn't happen to me. But seeing a little girl come at you—and that look she had in her eyes—"

"Yeah, the devil's messed up. But using little girls is not his most powerful play. It's the other stuff you've gotta watch out for."

"Other stuff? I didn't think it got any worse than controlling a kid."

"It's despicable, and sick, and twisted, but it's obvious. What you really have to be wary of is when he gets inside your head."

"Are you saying I'm at risk of being possessed?"

"Possessed? Nah. But that doesn't mean he can't destroy you from the inside out. When he talks to you in your own voice, that's when you have to be worried."

"Are you serious? I'm pretty sure I'd be freaked out if I heard my voice talking to me."

"You think so? How do you feel about yourself right now?"

"What do you mean?"

"Do you think you've got a great future ahead of you?"

"I can't think about anything accept defeating Julian. That's been my whole focus."

"Let's say we defeat Julian. Then what?"

"I have no idea."

"Do you think you deserve to live a good life after that?"

Eva's lips flattened. "I have no expectation of living a good life. Not after what I've done."

"But Jesus forgave you."

"Sure."

"But you haven't forgiven yourself."

"How can I?"

Clara slapped her leg. "Exactly. See?"

"No. I'm not following you at all."

"In your mind, you tell yourself you don't deserve to be forgiven."

"Yeah."

"You think Jesus is wrong to forgive you?"

"I think he's more generous than I am."

"In the Bible, it says that the devil is the accuser of the brethren. You reckon when you tell yourself you can't be forgiven that it's *you* saying those things?"

"It is."

Clara growled. "You want to know how you can defeat Julian? You need to believe God."

"I do."

"The devil wants you to fail, so he tells you that everything Jesus did for you is for nothing. If you don't let him forgive you, you destroy the power of the cross. That voice in your head"—Clara jabbed a pudgy finger in Eva's direction—"is not connected to the spirit of God that lives inside of you now. Otherwise, that voice in your head would be in agreement with Jesus."

"How do you know that?"

"Are you serious?" Clara shook her head. "And they say my theology is messed up."

"Lynn and I haven't had much time together. I'm doing the best I can with limited understanding."

"Sorry. You're right. I of all people should know better than to give you a hard time. Let me lay it out for you. When you accepted Jesus, you had every single sin forgiven. Everything. Every evil thing you did is forgiven."

"Lynn told me that."

"The Bible also says that we are a new creation. You aren't the person you were."

"But I still struggle with the stuff I grew up believing."

"Yeah. No kiddin'. That's 'cause it's a journey. You don't have to be perfect, but you will have to let go of your past and let God work on you. And when that voice in your head—that sounds like you—starts telling you lies, you tell it to shut up."

Eva smiled. "The devil doesn't like to be told to shut up?"

"He thinks he's somethin' special. You need to remind him that he's got nothin' on you. He'll accuse you like it says in the Bible, but it's up to you to not listen. You can trust me on this. I'm an expert at believing the lies I tell myself. The devil makes us our own worst enemy."

"I'll try my best."

"And one last thing."

"Yeah?"

"Don't go running off like you did. That was stupid."

"I know. I already promised Ben. I'm sorry. I made a

mistake going after Katy, but I won't stop praying for her."

"Good. So what are your thoughts on this Mr. Lyons fellow?"

"I'm waiting to hear what Ben has to say."

"But what's your gut telling you?"

"If my gut can be relied upon, then I believe he's definitely our next move."

The burner phone rang and Eva answered. "Lynn, I've got you on speaker. How's it going?"

"I spoke to Sarah."

"I hope you have good news."

"She was surprised by what I told her."

"She should be. Did she say she'd vote against the bill?"

"Eva, she was surprised that I'd joined the ranks of those *crazy conspiracy theorists*. Her words. Not mine."

Clara huffed. "Everyone's a cynic."

"Does that mean she's voting yes?"

"I'm going to keep working on her. I get the feeling there's more going on than we know."

"All right, well, keep at it. In the meantime, move through the list as best as you can."

"Where are you guys at with Lyons?"

"I'm waiting to see how the others feel about it." She looked at Clara.

"All I'm getting from the Almighty is that we don't need to fear. He keeps saying he's with us. It's not much to go on, but it's all he's givin' me."

"Eva, you really believe he'd move against Julian?"

"Even if we get him on our side, it will still be a big risk for him. I won't know unless I speak to him."

"Then we better get moving," Ben said from the door. Eva looked up at him and he nodded. "I'm confident about moving on Lyons."

"Keep me updated," Lynn said. "And stay safe."

"You too." Eva tucked the phone back in her pocket. "Does that mean we're all in agreement?"

"Sounds like it. Has Lynn spoken with Sarah yet?"

"Yeah. She didn't get a positive response. Lynn's going to keep working on her and the others."

"Okay, so how do we approach Lyons?"

"We'll need to get him alone."

"And what's the chance he'll alert Julian without hearing us out first?"

"There's a chance, but it's small. He's always liked me."

"But you betrayed Julian."

"I still think he'd listen."

"How much time do we need?"

"I won't know until we talk to him. I don't know how much convincing he'll need. We should be able to find him at his house tonight."

Clara groaned. "Nighttime again? Why does everything have to happen at night?"

"It will take us a few hours to get to his place anyway."

"Does he have much security?" Ben said.

"I plan on walking in the front door."

"You think he'll let us in?"

"Not us. Me."

"I won't let you go alone again."

"You can come." She stood and slapped his arm as she walked past him. "You just can't go in the front door. You won't be invited in."

Julian found Katy sitting silently on her bed when he entered the room. She had a red mark on her cheek.

"You want to tell me what happened?" he said, sitting down beside her.

"Bea already told you."

"But I want to hear your side of the story. Bea said Harold told you Eva was coming."

"Yes."

"You didn't think it was important to let any of us know?"

"Harold said not to. He told me I was big enough to handle it myself."

"And Bea doesn't believe you?"

"No."

"Is that why she slapped you?"

Katy sucked in her cheeks.

"Katy?"

"When she said she didn't believe me, I said she should ask Harold herself."

"I see. Is that all you said?"

"It wasn't me, it was Harold."

"But you're the one who spoke the words. What else did you say?"

"That Harold didn't speak to her anymore because

he didn't care about her anymore. He said she was old and useless."

"Why would you say that to Bea?"

"I told you, it wasn't me. He told me she was an old hag. He said she was never as powerful as I would be one day."

Julian cleared his throat. "Do you think that was a good reason to let your training go out the window?"

"My training?"

"When is it a good time to attack someone with words in the way you did to Bea?"

"She treats me like a little girl. Harold treats me better. I was mad."

"And you know that when you're angry, that is when you need to have extra control. You don't want to undo everything you've taken the time to build up. Besides, Bea has been very good to you and it was wrong of you to speak to her that way."

"I'm sorry."

"I'm not the one you need to apologize to."

"I know," she mumbled.

Julian took a breath. He had more important things he needed to find out from Katy. "So. You thought you could take on Eva on your own?"

She bounced beside him, becoming animated. "I'm not lying. Harold said I could. I believed him. He's never lied to me before."

"You think he lied to you then?"

Katy frowned in thought. "I don't know."

"What do your instincts tell you?"

"I don't think he was lying."

"But you did attack her?"

"Yeah, but she was stronger. I don't know why."

"Eva is a grown woman who's been trained to fight her whole life."

"Yeah, but Harold said I would be stronger. He said he'd help me."

"Did you feel stronger?"

"Well…"

"What is it?"

"I don't really remember."

"What do you mean?"

"I remember jumping. It was almost like I was pushed, but then I sort of…I can't remember anything until she pushed me off."

"Were you scared?"

"No. I was confused."

"Did you tell Bea about blacking out?"

Her head dropped. "No. I didn't want to get into more trouble."

Julian ran his hand down the back of her head. "All right. You stay here for now. I'll go have a chat with Bea and see if we can't get this whole thing straightened out."

"Thanks, Uncle Julian."

"Next time, if Harold tells you to do something and says not to tell, will you let me know and I'll have a chat with him?"

She shook her head. "I can't."

"Why not?"

She scrunched up her face. "'Cause he's the one who's in charge. Not you."

Julian squeezed his fingers into his palm as he fought for control. He'd done what Bea had asked and opened up to this spirit she followed, but Katy was his and he didn't like being pushed aside for some ethereal thing with no substance other than what the flesh gave to him.

"Stay here," he said abruptly and left the room to find Bea.

He found her reading a book in one of the studies. "I spoke to Katy."

"You disagree with my harsh reaction?"

"I think you lost control, but she shouldn't have said what she did."

"I have never given out discipline without a steady hand. She got what she deserved. She was disrespectful."

Julian's laugh was cold. "It's your own fault. You created a monster you don't like."

"Excuse me?"

"She said she blacked out when she attacked Eva. I don't understand how this works, but it sounds to me like Harold possessed her."

Bea sighed. "She didn't tell me that part."

"If he has control over her, you can't blame her when she passes on a message."

"So she's invited him in."

"Are you surprised?"

"I shouldn't be."

"All I want to know is if it's a good or a bad thing. Do we need to intervene?"

"Of course not. This is good. However…"

"What?"

"If Harold did expect to subdue Eva, then why couldn't he?"

"Maybe he's not as strong as you think."

Bea threw the book aside. "You still don't believe."

"I'm not sure what it is I'm supposed to believe, but I'd be happier about Harold's presence if he was respectful enough to keep me informed. I don't like being kept in the dark in my own home."

"But this isn't your home. This was Harold's home and he is still here, which means the house still belongs to him."

"Unless Asmodeus disagrees? Or are they one and the same?"

Bea laughed. "Please don't tell me you're planning on attempting to influence him in your favor?"

"Harold has no power except what Katy has given him. If she didn't let him use her, he'd be nothing."

"Can I give you a piece of advice?"

"Sure."

"Don't mess with powers you don't understand. Be obedient, do your part, and you'll be rewarded. But if you step out of line, there are consequences."

"Is that a threat?"

"Yes, but it's not from me."

"After all these years, why is it you are only now revealing your true colors? What's changed?"

"Nothing has changed. If you don't like the turn things have taken, don't complain to me about it. I've always been loyal to the cause."

"The problem I have is that you always said you were loyal to me."

"I'm sorry you got that impression. It was incorrect. I did not do it to deceive you. But if we are both loyal to the same cause, then there should be no problem."

"I'm not so sure anymore that they are the same."

"Has it ever crossed your mind that perhaps it's you that's moving off course? It only takes a small deviation."

"And if I have?"

"I've already told you. If you want to win, you must submit."

Julian scoffed.

"I know you don't like it. But you're lucky he thinks highly of you. He hasn't given up on you yet."

"What does that mean?"

"It means he'd still like you to be a part of this. To show his gratitude for the work you've already put in and as a show of good faith, he has a gift to give you."

"What kind of gift?"

"It's a gift that represents your last chance. Receive it with grace and put aside your pride. Trust him. Let him lead you and you will conquer all."

"If he's so powerful, he should be able to give me Eva. She is the only gift I will accept that will earn my unwavering support."

"That's what he's offering."

"You're kidding. He can tell me where to find her?"

"He can. So you submit?"

"Where is she?"

Clara smiled. "Don't say such things lightly. He will take you at your word."

"I'm not being light. If I can get rid of Eva, I can

finally move forward with confidence without having to wait for her next move. Now tell me where she is."

"Clara Palmer."

"What about her?"

"You may want to pay her a visit."

"Where? The FBI said she'd escaped."

"Every bird returns to its nest."

"You think she can help?"

"She's harboring your enemy."

"If this is true, then why didn't he tell me before?"

"Asmodeus is powerful, but he's not omniscient. No being can know everything. He's been searching for her and now he's found her. Do you want her or not?"

Chapter 22

CONGRESSMAN MARCUS LYONS unbuttoned his suit coat before pouring himself a stiff drink. He swished the brown contents of the glass before sitting on the large leather sofa where he propped his feet on the coffee table. It had been a long day that had caused suppressed memories to resurface. Memories that had been long buried and should have stayed that way, but over the last week everywhere he looked he was reminded of past sins that he thought he had excused away.

The doorbell rang and he listened as the footsteps of his bodyguard approached the front door. It was probably overcautious of him to keep a bodyguard around, but he'd been increasingly uneasy, and when Julian had made the offer of protection, he reluctantly conceded. It did give him a small amount of comfort, but no bodyguard could stop the thoughts that had been plaguing him every night.

A soft knock came at the door.

"Yes?"

"I'm sorry to bother you, sir, but there is a reporter at the door."

He pinched the bridge of his nose. "Get rid of them. That's the last thing I want to deal with tonight."

"She said you'd want to see her."

Lyons stomach twisted. If she was here to blackmail him, she'd be out of luck. He had nothing left to offer that hadn't already been taken. Julian had everything on him that was worth having. Pretending to still be a close friend only twisted the knife.

"Tell her I'm sleeping."

"She said she expected you to refuse her entry."

"Then why did she bother turning up?"

"She wanted me to let you know her name was Eva."

Lyons nearly spilled his drink as a tremor shook him. He set the glass on the table and tightened his hand into a fist.

He swallowed before speaking so he could be sure to get the words out of his mouth. "Show her in, please."

Standing, he buttoned his coat, staring at the door until Eva walked through.

She looked different from the last time he'd seen her. She had always carried herself like she was going to war, but even though she looked battle weary, a liberation steadied her gaze. He'd admired her for escaping Julian, even though he'd never admit it. But the woman who stood before him was now an unknown quantity and he couldn't imagine why she was here, except for perhaps extracting her revenge for his connection to Julian. But whatever the purpose of her visit, he could never defend himself against her. He'd rather she beat him to death than ever lay a finger on her.

"Eva. It's been a long time."

"Marcus. I don't know whether to say it's good to see you or not."

"I'm glad to see we have at least that in common tonight."

He watched as she walked past him to the glass doors that led outside. She opened them, and a man walked in.

Marcus opened his mouth to call for his bodyguard, but the man held his hands up to show he had no weapon.

"This is my friend Ben. We're not here to hurt you. We want to talk."

Lyons looked at the two and found he wasn't as afraid as he'd expected to be. But Eva had no threat to offer that would be worse than what he currently suffered. "Would you like to sit?"

"Thank you."

He moved to a chair to allow his uninvited guests to sit together on the couch.

"Can I get either of you a drink?" he said, reaching for his own.

"No, we're fine," Eva said.

"Did Julian send you? I heard you were back with him, but wasn't sure what to think."

"That was short-lived and only because I lost my memory for a time."

"You escaped him a second time?"

"I did. With Ben's help."

"You have more luck than anyone else I know."

"It wasn't luck."

"Call it what you will, but if you're not here for Julian, why are you here?"

"The terror bill you're about to vote on."

"What about it?"

"We need to stop it."

Lyons shook his head. "You've wasted your time coming here. There's nothing I can do to help you."

"You can change your vote. You have a lot of sway."

"I can't."

"Marcus, I know you haven't always agreed with Julian's methods. If you knew what he was planning, you'd stand against him in this. It's your chance to do the right thing."

Lyons smiled sadly and sipped his drink. "You always had a way of reading people. If you knew how I felt, why didn't you report me to Julian?"

"I was having my own misgivings at the time, and I've always considered you a friend."

"I'm glad you could get free of him, but we aren't all as lucky as you. I don't have the same luxury."

"With all due respect, sir," Ben said. "We need to stop this bill, no matter the cost. If it goes through...you must know that Julian is ready to take advantage of it. Do you really want to give him that kind of power?"

"He already has that kind of power. That's why the bill will pass. There's no way to stop it."

"I can't blame you for being fatalistic," Eva said. "But we can't give up now. We haven't lost everything yet. Julian isn't invincible."

"What makes you think you can stop him? He's got influence over too many people."

"Influence, yes, but not loyalty. Most of the people voting on that bill are being coerced in his favor. If enough people stand up against him, he can be stopped. Imagine how much worse it will be if we do nothing."

"And you think you'll succeed?"

"Who better than his own daughter to bring his reign to an end?"

Lyons blanched and Eva must have noticed because she scooted forward on the couch.

"What is it? You really don't think we have a chance? I'm his own flesh and blood. I know how he thinks and what he wants. There's a cost to all of us, but it's worth it."

There was an innocence about her that frightened him. When she was under Julian's spell, she was cold. It made it easy to forget how young she was. Now she had a light inside her that he wished he couldn't sense. It was too bright and clear to ignore.

"It never occurred to me you didn't know," he said.

"Didn't know what?"

"There's nothing I regret more than trusting Julian in the first place. I was too preoccupied with my own pride and desires to see what was really going on. He always looked for the best and the brightest. Set up training facilities all over the country so he could monitor them from afar, but he always wanted to find the one he could keep the closest, one that could carry on his name…I thought you knew."

Eva's face was tight. "Knew what?"

He watched as Ben moved his hand slowly and placed it on her leg. He'd figured it out even though she struggled to allow the truth any room.

"This may not——" Lyons pushed his hand down his pant leg. It should be a comfort for Eva to know she wasn't really Julian's child. But the ramifications went beyond the man she thought was her father, and they would cause this woman who he had known as a little girl deeper wounds than she already had. "Julian had no biological children."

Eva crushed her lips together, pinning them between her teeth.

"I'm sorry. I thought you knew. But the best thing you can do is walk out of here and live your life. He's already done enough to you. Don't let him have any more of your time."

"You know for sure that Julian is not my real father?"

"Yes."

"How long have you known?"

"Always. I respected him once. We were young men when I met him. His ideas for the future were grand, and he offered me a front-row seat. It was great for a while. Julian already knew people. Powerful people. And I liked being on the inside. I was getting into politics and it was the first time anyone actually listened to my ideas...or at least they pretended to. I don't even know when it changed. It was small things at first. I remember when he brought you home. He introduced you to me as his daughter, and it scared me. Somehow I hadn't noticed how bad it had gotten and by then it was too late. I wanted to rescue you and I've always felt guilty for not doing something."

"But why me?"

He couldn't help her, but he hated to let her down. If she went after Julian, she'd lose. Maybe if he hurt her, she'd back off. It would break his heart, but he meant what he said to her. She needed to go off and live her life.

"You were no different from the rest, except your test scores were the highest. He saw the potential in you and took you for his own."

"Like the girl he has now. Are my parents still alive?"

"I don't know."

"I want to know."

"I told you, I don't know."

"You must have known something about it."

"Your parents were drug addicts. He told them he would take you to a special boarding school for gifted children in exchange for supplying them with drugs."

"So my parents sold me? They didn't notice when I never returned?"

"I'm sure they thought they were doing what was best for you."

"But they never came looking for me?"

"The drugs Julian supplied them were supposed to kill them. I don't know any more than that."

Eva stared at the wall.

"I'm so sorry," Ben said, moving his hand to her shoulder.

Marcus saw the connection between the two. It was

a weakness they couldn't afford. Julian would use everything against them if they tried to take him on.

Eva sniffed back the tears that threatened but didn't fall. "I guess that's good news for me. I'm relieved knowing he's not my real father."

"I'd hoped you'd find it positive in some small way. I hope it helps you move on with your life."

"No. I won't move on with my life until I stop Julian. I helped him get to where he is and I will do whatever it takes to stop that bill."

"This isn't your responsibility. You need to let this go. You won't stop him."

"I don't agree. We still have a chance. And if you have the guts to change your vote, you can finally do the right thing."

He stood to refill his glass. "Why are you bothering with me? I'm only one person."

"But you have a lot of influence. I know there are those who will follow you."

He gripped his glass so tightly his hand shook. "You don't know what you're asking of me," he said, keeping his back to her.

"I know exactly what I'm asking of you."

"I can't do it."

"You really want to live in a world where Julian is in control?"

He spun around and raised his voice. "I already do. My life is hell. Every day is hell. Do you know what it's like knowing that every move you make is controlled by someone else?"

"Yes. I do."

"I'm sorry. You're right. But you're stronger than I am."

"That's not true. I know you, Marcus. You care."

He scoffed. "The biggest weakness of all. It's the reason you'll fail."

"No. It's the reason we'll succeed. It's those of us who know what Julian truly is who can break his hold. You know as well as I do that he's mad and we are both responsible for supporting his madness. We've kept it going longer than we should have, and we have to answer for that. Julian is as powerful as he is because we've allowed him to become that. It's our fault. So now we have to fix it."

"It's too late."

"We can't know that until we've exhausted all options. It's our duty to sacrifice ourselves to stop him. We have to stop protecting ourselves. We're talking about the lives of potentially millions of people. Please, Marcus. I'm here because I know that deep down you want to do what's right. You want to be free from Julian, and that's what I'm offering you today. Freedom. Real, true freedom."

"How can you expect me to give up on my life in one night?"

"This is living? Being afraid and controlled is how you want to finish your life? Your whole life you've been following his orders, knowing that it's wrong. I've known you long enough to be sure that's never what you wanted."

"I don't know." A small spark of hope ignited inside him. He wanted Julian to lose. He had for a long time.

Knowing there were people trying to stop him filled Marcus with a longing he'd never dared feel before.

"We don't have a lot of time," Ben said. "But right now we're just talking. So, hypothetically speaking, if you decided to vote against the bill, how many people do you think you could turn?"

Lyons ran a finger across his mouth and looked at Ben. "I know Eva's connection to Julian. What's yours?"

"I used to work for him."

"Doing what?"

"Whatever needed doing. Mostly as a bodyguard or anything that needed strength and skill."

"Why did you leave him?"

"I never fully understood what he was doing. Once I did, that changed everything."

"One of the good ones, huh? Not like the rest of us who got in so deep we could never recover. I didn't think your kind existed. But then, I never would have expected Eva to change."

"We all have that opportunity."

"Hypothetically speaking, Hoak, Sullivan, and Rodriguez would follow immediately. Julian has nothing on them. He had me influence their decision. If I tell them I've swapped sides, I'm sure they'll come with me. They're only interested in a good argument. Once they follow, there's others they could speak to." He wasn't ready to fully commit yet, but if he could get the names out there, perhaps it would boost his confidence.

"Great," Eva said. "That's what we want. The chain reaction."

"Butler and Crane. I think we could get them to turn."

"That's good. Thank you for trusting me with this."

"If you were anyone else…I remember pushing you on the swing when you were a little girl."

"I remember too."

"You were a talented little girl, sure. It was clear there was something different about you, but at the same time, there was this joy that you had. Julian didn't deserve it."

"I don't know if you're remembering correctly. From what I recall, I was a very serious child."

"You were serious, sure, but I think that was your empathy. You were surrounded by so much darkness. It affected you and Julian tried to train it out of you, but I can see now that it's still there. You brought it back." He could see his comments affected her. He was glad he had the opportunity to share them with her.

"Thank you for that," she said.

"No matter what happens, I want you to know that it has been a gift seeing that you truly are free from him."

Eva stood from the couch and walked over to him. He wasn't expecting it, and when she wrapped her arms around him and squeezed, he knew he'd do whatever it took to help her succeed.

Chapter 23

JULIAN BUTTONED his coat when he got out of the car. The property was quieter than last time and he wondered for a moment if Asmodeus had sent him on a wild-goose chase. But it didn't feel abandoned. He couldn't be certain Eva was here, but he was confident they'd get their hands on Clara.

"There's an underground bunker inside. The entrance is in the main bedroom closet," he said to Tyler.

"Did Bea tell you that?"

"You don't trust me?"

"I like to know our information is reliable."

"Actually, Eva told me."

"Was this before or after she knocked me unconscious and helped our prisoner escape?"

Julian swung around and gripped Tyler's throat. He didn't squeeze, but Tyler was smart enough to stand still.

"I thought we already went through this. If you had killed her in the first place, we wouldn't have any of this mess to clean up. I took a chance bringing her home, and as with any risk, there are uncertainties. In this case, things didn't pan out. But if you are going to continue to question my decisions—" He pulled a gun from his jacket and pressed it against Tyler's cheek. "I can kill you now and save myself the trouble."

Tyler's eyes angled down toward the gun. "No, sir. That won't be necessary."

"Good." Julian released him and reholstered his gun. "Eva spoke about it in her sleep. That's how I know. Clear the house, then check for the door to the bunker. If there isn't one there, then we know the information is incorrect and we will move forward accordingly."

"Yes, sir."

"And, Tyler."

"Sir?"

"I want zero casualties. Whoever is in there is coming out alive or don't bother coming out yourself."

"Sir."

Tyler gathered half the men to enter the house with him and ordered the other half to check the perimeter.

Several minutes later, a gunshot broke the still air. The men outside ran for the house.

Julian knew the shot wasn't fired from any of the guns his men had. If Eva was in there, she was putting up a fight. He wouldn't expect anything less.

A shrill scream was followed by thunderous banging, then the group exited the house, dragging a heavy woman who thrashed around like electricity was surging through her body.

Julian smiled and walked toward the group as

another of his guys hopped out the door with his hand pressed against his leg.

Tyler threw Clara to the ground, where she landed hard enough to stop her bucking. When she tried to rise, he yanked her arm behind her. "Shut up and lay still."

She roared and pushed back, but he pressed his knee into her. "I could break your arm if you want to be difficult."

She grunted and finally settled when he twisted harder.

"Clara," Julian said as he sauntered closer. "I expected better hospitality from a country woman such as yourself. I believe you shot one of my men."

Clara screwed her head around so she could get a look at him. "You guys are trespassing. Didn't you read the sign when you drove in here? It says trespassers will be shot. I did warn you."

He crouched down so he could look into her face more easily. "We didn't mean to upset you."

She spat at him and Tyler made her regret it. She squirmed, dipping her head to the ground and arching her back to keep her arm from snapping.

Julian waited for her to catch her breath before he continued. "My apologies for barging in like this, but I'm looking for someone important to me. I have reason to believe that my daughter, Eva, is staying with you, or you know where she is."

"Why would I tell you anything?"

Tyler raised his arm to hit her, but Julian stopped him. "There's no need for that. You can't blame her for her reaction to our intrusion. But, Clara, Eva is a traitor, and it is imperative that I find her. She's turned against me."

"I know."

"I must say, I'm shocked at your response." He sniffed. "She did send your son to prison, after all."

"He sent himself to prison."

Julian couldn't keep the ironic smile from curling up the side of his face. "Eva was always good at making people believe whatever she wanted."

"It won't work," Clara croaked. "I know all about you. You are a vile, horrible man. You can do what you want to me, but you'll never get what you want."

He reached out and wiped a smudge of dirt from her cheek. "Sweetheart, when I'm done with you, you will beg to kill Eva yourself."

"Then you underestimate me."

"I guess we'll find out. But first we're going to have a look around, if you don't mind."

"Of course I mind."

"Right. Because this property you own is private and legally we have no right to search it."

"I know my rights. I might not like the police much, but at least they don't come barging in without a warrant."

"And that's the rub. We aren't law-abiding citizens. You should be grateful we didn't shoot you first."

Clara scoffed. "Thanks for your kindness, but I'm sure you'll get around to it once I'm no longer useful to you."

"I do what is necessary in order to get the outcome required. Ultimately, I only want what's best for humanity and that comes at a cost. But I consider myself to be a gentleman and prefer to do things in an orderly manner, including gaining your permission to continue searching your property."

"You won't find anything. I live alone."

"Then you have nothing to worry about." Julian stepped back and looked over at the man who had been shot. He looked pale. "Will one of you take him to get that fixed up before I have another dead body I need to dispose of? The rest of you keep looking. And kill any livestock you find."

"You can't do that," Clara squealed.

"Then tell me where I can find Eva."

"No. I won't do it."

"Then consider it an act of mercy. You won't be coming back from where you're going, so they'd all starve anyway. Tyler, tie her up and put her in the trunk."

"You can't—" Tyler kicked her in the side to shut her up.

Julian flinched. "I appreciate your enthusiasm, but don't overdo it. We need her in reasonable condition."

"Yes, sir." Tyler dragged her across the yard and shoved her in the trunk. She put up a small struggle, but it was clear she'd lost her fight.

Julian went inside the house to look around.

Tyler joined him. "We've already confirmed there is no one else present in the house, but there are signs that more than one person is living here."

"Have you found anything that points directly to Eva?"

"Not yet."

"What about the papers Michael said she retrieved from the office?"

"We haven't found those yet either."

"I want this place turned upside down. We need to find out what they're up to and what they know."

Tyler's phone rang.

"It's Brant," he said before answering. "Yeah?" He listened and then looked at Julian. "Don't make a move until we arrive." He hung up. "There's been a development."

Ben had said little during the exchange. He knew it was important for Eva to make a personal connection to Lyons in order to gain his trust. She'd done it, but he could see on her face that it had cost her.

She gave Ben a small nod when she returned to the couch, but the smile on her face didn't reach her eyes. It had been an important encounter in more ways than one, and while she must have been relieved to discover Julian wasn't her biological father, it posed a new opportunity for pain, knowing that her parents were murdered by a man who pretended to care for her.

"You're making the right choice," Ben said.

Lyons lifted his glass to take a drink, but set it back on the counter and pushed it away. "One thing I've learned over the years is that 'right' is a relative term. What is right for one is wrong for another. It's all about choosing sides and hoping you've picked the best one."

Eva shook her head. "The reason I could leave Julian wasn't simply deciding I believed the other side over his. I discovered there is an ultimate truth. We get lost in moral ambiguities because we don't want to accept the truth. But firm boundaries are necessary to sustain life and freedom."

"But not all boundaries are good."

"Exactly."

Lyons squinted at Eva. "What is this discovery you made?"

"I found God."

The shock on Lyons's face was unmistakable. "You gave up worshiping Julian in exchange for some god?"

"Not *some* god. *The* God."

"And which one is that?"

"The Christian one."

"You mean Jesus?"

"Yeah."

Lyons scrambled for his glass and took a big gulp, grimacing as it burned down his throat. "I must be a madman following a woman who's swapped one prophet for another."

Ben watched Eva to see what her next move would be. He had to trust her on this. She knew Lyons and he did not.

Movement at the door diverted his attention. He saw the gun before anyone else, and at the first shot, he dove for Eva, yanking her to the floor.

Glass shattered somewhere nearby. Ben pulled out his weapon as he scrambled across the floor to get a clear shot of the assailant who approached their position. He fired before the man could attack. A thud indicated he'd found his mark.

Jumping up to a crouch, he checked to make sure the man was dead and quickly retrieved the gun from his hand.

Eva appeared beside him briefly before hurrying over to where Lyons laid dead on the floor.

"Marcus." She laid her head on his chest. "I'm so sorry. This isn't what I wanted."

"Eva, we have to go now." He tried to pull her backward, but she shrugged him off. "Eva. We don't have time. We have to get out of here now." He tightened his grip and pulled. She finally gave in and he led her to the door at the back of the room.

She stumbled blindly along with him as he directed her away from the property. "The man who shot Lyons. Do you know who that was?"

"He answered the door. Not a butler. A bodyguard, I think."

"He must work for Julian."

"I should have known. I knew it was a risk, but I didn't expect that. I thought we were the ones in danger, not the men and woman voting on the bill. Julian has no problem killing someone, but he doesn't do it without cause. Marcus hadn't even turned against him yet."

"We don't know that Julian ordered the hit, but we can't stick around to find out."

"I don't know how I'd been blinded for so many years. How I couldn't see what Julian really was. That he wasn't really my father. I don't even remember my parents."

"You were a little girl. Probably too small to remember."

"What if he had never found me? What if I had the chance to grow up normal?"

"Your parents were drug addicts."

"And you think that's worse?"

"I don't know what your life could have been, but one thing I do know is that if Julian never trained you, you wouldn't be equipped to stop him now. You wouldn't be here and I'd probably be dead. If we're going to survive this, we can't focus on what could have been or we'll go mad. All we can do is look forward."

"But every time it looks like we get a win, Julian is there to destroy the progress we've made."

"He hasn't destroyed it." They reached the truck and Ben pulled the passenger door open, but Eva didn't get in. "We lost Lyons and it's okay to grieve for him. But then we have to keep moving. We have more names now."

He was saying all the things he knew he should, but as much as he said them to comfort Eva, he struggled to believe the words he spoke. The hardest thing they were going to face at the end of all of this was to not let the hate take over. If they did, Julian would still win.

Julian rested his hand on his hip as he looked down at the two corpses. "I thought you told him to wait," he said to Tyler, who was checking Lyons's pockets.

"I did."

Julian lifted a small statue beside him. It was heavy. He hurled it across the room, where it smashed against the wall.

They'd had yet another break, but Eva continued to elude them. "Is the team in place at Clara's in case they return there?"

"Yes, sir."

He'd given in to Bea's suggestion that he yield to Asmodeus, but despite his words to her, he had refused to recognize the supernatural power as having any truly remarkable effect. But it was impossible for Eva to remain out of reach without help that went beyond the natural. He was finding it harder to avoid the truth he dreaded—that Asmodeus was the one in control, and if he didn't give in, he'd forfeit everything he'd worked so hard for.

Chapter 24

EVA SQUEEZED her knees as they drove back to Clara's.

"We have names," she said. "You're right. We lost Marc—we had a setback, but we need to focus on what we gained. I'll call Lynn and—"

"Eva, stop."

"What'd you mean, stop? You said yourself that we have to keep moving forward. I know Rodriguez. Julian's got some stuff on him, but when I tell him what happened to Marcus, he'll side with us. I'll get an update from Lynn and see how she's coming along. She might have more names for us as well."

Ben's jaw tightened. "Eva, if you don't process this stuff, it sticks with you. It will follow you around and you don't need that."

"Process what stuff? You just said we can't dwell on the past."

"That's not what I meant, and you know it. Someone you were close to was murdered in front of you. Not to mention that you found out tonight that Julian isn't your real father. You can't ignore that."

"I'm not ignoring it. I'm moving on. Marcus Lyons was a part of Julian's team from way back. He's been a part of the Underwood Foundation's plans from the start and he knew the risks. And as for Julian not being my father, it's like you said, things have turned out the way they're supposed to."

Ben gripped the wheel with both hands. He processed several different versions of the same sentence, but in the end he said nothing. Eva was right. He'd just finished telling her to move forward and forget the past, and here he was telling her to focus on it. He leaned forward to look up at the dark sky. Maybe this is what Felix was talking about when he told Ben not to try to fix her.

"You don't need to worry about me, okay?" Eva said, turning as far away from Ben as she could. "It's not worth your time or energy."

"This isn't what I wanted," he mumbled.

"You think it's what I wanted? We both understood going in that a happy ending was not in store for either of us. We both came in broken and no matter what the outcome is, there's no coming back from this."

"Does it have to be like that?"

"Yes. It does. We're giving everything because neither one of us has anything to lose. Do I hate that Lyons died? Yes. Do I hate Julian for ruining my life? Yes. But even though I have weak moments of regret and pain, everything that you said before is right. We have to stay focused on stopping Julian. There's no room for anything else."

"I thought we were doing it because we're following God."

"Same thing. You think if you had a family at home, you'd be here now?"

He looked at Eva, then quickly looked back at the road. If she was the one at home waiting for him, she was right. He wouldn't want to be out here right now. "I don't know. But I hope there is something left for us at the end of this."

"And if not?"

"Either way, we get eternity in heaven. But I would like to see you happy."

"Why? What difference does it make to you?"

He grimaced in frustration. "Forget it."

Eva's voice was soft and low, but her words filled the truck. "We both know nothing can happen between us."

"So you admit there's something."

"No. There's nothing. There can be nothing. Don't you understand? We watched a man die because of us and you had to drag me away because I cared. It's a weakness that we can't afford. Not in this war."

"Fine. You want to wallow alone inside that pit that's eating you alive, then have a nice swim in there."

"Ben, come on. Tell me I'm wrong."

He couldn't.

He would have stopped the truck and gotten out to burn off some of the fire that had flared up inside him if he thought it would do him any good. Eva had a way of scrambling him until he didn't know which way was up.

He knew she was right. Nothing could happen between them, but he didn't want to accept it. He wasn't ready to give up on anything good coming out of this. But if his feelings for her put her life at risk, the best thing he could do was let it go.

Eva leaned her head back on the seat as they drove silently. What was it that Ben expected from her? She could barely admit to herself that she longed to let him in, but with so much inside that she was too scared to face, it was impossible. What did he think he could do for her there, anyway? The only thing she could offer him was brokenness. She hadn't been a Christian long, but she knew Jesus was the only one who had the power to deal with her darkness. He was the only one who knew what was going on deep inside in the dark places even she couldn't see into.

Her eyes drifted out of focus as fatigue began to take hold on the straight, dark road. But when a figure appeared out of nowhere in the headlights, she jerked upright as Ben slammed on the brakes.

The truck skidded to a halt with less than an inch of room to spare. The man, illuminated by the lights, looked distracted as he rested his hand on the hood.

Ben jumped out and slammed the door. "Felix, what are you doing? I could have hit you!" He shook his head. "You know what I mean."

"Get back in the truck," Felix said before walking around to Eva's side of the car. She had gotten out but had remained behind the door. "Eva," he said, getting into the back seat.

"What are you doing here?" she said after shutting her door.

"You can't go back to Clara's."

"Why?" Ben said. "What's happened? Is she in trouble?"

"I'm sorry." Felix folded his hands in his lap.

"Julian found her?" Eva said.

"Yes."

"Then we have to go save her."

"It's too late."

"No. It can't be too late. Why would you come tell us now when we can't help her? Why did you let us leave her there?"

"Because you have your path to walk and she has hers. Get back on the highway and get off at the third exit. There is a motel there called Cedar Lodge."

"Hang on a minute. Forget the motel. You need to tell us where to find her."

"Third exit. The man at the desk—"

"Felix!" Eva slammed her hand on the seat. "You got us away from Michael, you saved Ben from a burning building, you can help us rescue Clara."

"No."

"Are you saying there's nothing we can do?"

"There is plenty to do. Saving her is not one of them."

Eva and Ben looked at each other. Ben was the one to voice what they were both wondering. "Is she alive?"

"That doesn't matter."

"How can you say that?"

"You can't save her."

"Please," Eva begged.

"You're both struggling with this, but you have to trust me. Get on the highway. Third exit. Cedar Lodge."

"We don't have any money." Eva could barely get the words out, but she wanted him to understand that what he expected from them was ridiculous.

"Tell the man who's on duty your names. He'll give you a room."

"Felix——" Ben said.

"No! You need to listen. It's important." It was the first time Eva had heard Felix raise his voice.

She squeezed her eyes closed as she pinched the bridge of her nose. "Clara doesn't deserve this." When she opened her eyes, the back seat was empty. Eva slammed her hand on the seat again. "How can he expect us to forget about her?"

Ben was staring out the front window, but he lifted his gaze to the rearview where Felix was a moment ago.

"He didn't ask us to forget. He asked us to be obedient." Ben put the car into gear and planted his foot, burning rubber before the truck rumbled down the road.

"If he had told us sooner——"

"You heard him. She's got her path. We have ours," Ben said through clenched teeth. "What I'd like to know is how Julian knew where to find us."

"He would have been checking everywhere. It was probably a long shot, and he got lucky."

"But why even check there? It doesn't make sense

that we'd have sought shelter there in the first place. She was your enemy. He had no reason to look there. How could he know?"

"I don't know how he knew!" Eva buried her face in her hands. "I'm sorry. I'm just...I used to be better at this. I used to be able to remain unemotional."

"Emotion is not the enemy."

"Oh no? Since when?"

"What do we do when we want to give up?"

"Cry? Complain? Get angry?"

"Then what?"

"I'm not sure what you're after here. Give up?"

"Then what?"

"Ben."

"When we've got nothing left, we go to God and we say we've got nothing and we put all our reliance on him because we've got no answers and he does. And that's where we're at. We've got nothing. No hope except what God gives us. If we're going to win this, we need God to do it."

She blew out a long breath of air. "I'm so used to being in control."

"Me too. But that's the problem, isn't it? That's what we're trying to stop Julian from having."

"I don't know what we would do if we weren't both reliant on God."

Ben huffed a laugh. "Equally yoked."

"What?"

"It's what my mom used to say. She'd tell me you can't have a good marriage if you can't share the most fundamental part of your life with them."

"But we're not married."

"No, I didn't mean—It works in partnerships as well."

Eva frowned. "I've never asked you about your parents before."

"They're dead. Dad left when I was eight. Mom died in a car accident after I graduated from high school. Drunk driver."

"I'm so sorry."

"She was the drunk driver. Life's hard sometimes. She struggled in life herself, but she did leave me with a few good gems."

"We've both been left with no parents, and the only other person in our lives who is close, we can't do anything to help. It makes me feel so helpless and it breaks my heart."

"But we have to trust God. We have to believe he's with her. He can do more than we can, anyway. We have to believe in his plan even if we can't understand it. Even if we never do."

Eva was quiet, but when they pulled off the exit, she said, "If she's not dead already, he'll torture, then kill her."

Ben nodded. "But she's a strong woman. I don't think he'll be able to break her."

"That is a very cold comfort."

"I know, but there's nothing else we can do about it."

"There's one thing I can do." Eva bowed her head.

Chapter 25

JULIAN FLUNG BEA'S door open. Her hair, usually tied up in a bun, hung loosely at her shoulders. She pulled her robe more tightly around herself.

"Julian, what on earth?"

"Sorry, Bea, but I need your help."

Her lips pressed softly together. Julian only noticed because he noticed everything. She was pleased. It burned him, but he'd do what was necessary, even if it meant selling his soul to the devil himself.

"You know I'll do anything for you that is within my power." She swept over to the jewel-colored chaise lounge and sat like a queen.

This was a new side of Bea he hadn't seen before. The woman was usually more matronly and gracious. It worried him she might know more than she was letting on. But that didn't mean he couldn't put her in her place. "Don't you mean Asmodeus's power? You've shown me your hand and I now know who you really serve."

"That doesn't mean I don't retain some amount of loyalty toward you. You've been like a son to me most of my life, and that has only strengthened my care for you now. I only want what's best for you."

"As far as it lines up with Asmodeus's plans."

"His plan is best for you. For both of us."

"That suits me just fine right now, because I need Asmodeus to do something for me."

Bea sighed. "I hope you understand you cannot demand anything from him."

"My patience is already wearing very thin. I wouldn't ask if it wasn't in both of our best interests."

"Very well. What is it you would like him to do?"

"I'm tired of his games. I want him to kill Eva."

Bea tugged at her earlobe. "What happened to the last gift he gave you?"

"I found Clara, not Eva. He promised me Eva."

Bea straightened. "What do you mean?"

"We went to Clara's house and Eva wasn't there. She hasn't returned. So his *gift* was not what was promised."

"Did you do as I asked before? Did you give yourself over to him? Fully? As I instructed?"

"In a manner of speaking."

"In other words, no."

"I've been happy for him to be in charge, but surrendering myself to him is another matter."

She grinned. "You must feel foolish."

"You of all people know how I feel about being in control. You're asking me to give that up. That's not easy."

"That's one excuse."

"You believe there is another reason?"

"I do. A sophisticated man such as yourself speaking strange words into a mirror. It's ridiculous."

"You said it, not me."

"Your pride continues to keep you from reaching greater heights. You know I only want what is best for you. This is best."

"You're saying that if I indulge in his absurd rituals, he'll grant my request?"

"They appear absurd to you because you don't really believe."

"Can you blame me?"

"Yes, actually. He's proven himself and yet you still refuse to give in to the truth of his lordship. That is why Eva continues to elude you. You are playing games with him, so he is playing games with you. In the end, you can guess who will lose."

Julian sighed. "It's difficult for me."

"Only the first step is hard. After that, it becomes easy. You do this small thing and you'll see. Then we can ask him together if he will give you what you desire most and see what he has to say."

"Fine." Julian pointed at the gilded mirror hanging on the wall. "Will that one do?"

"Yes."

He walked up to the mirror and looked at Bea in the reflection. She leaned back against the couch with a satisfied smile.

"Is it appropriate for you to be here while I do this?" he said.

"Why not? It is my room, after all."

He focused back on himself, let out a breath, then recited the phrases she'd taught him when he was a boy. He didn't know the meaning of the words he spoke so it was odd that they came back into his memory so easily. Each syllable was as clear as the day Bea had first taught them to him. Back then, they'd sounded magical, but today he forced back the awkwardness of speaking gibberish as a grown man. The words gonged in his head and he gave in. If it wasn't real, it wouldn't do any harm, and if it was, he'd get what he wanted.

When he'd finished, his eyes refocused on Bea. "Is that it? Did I forget anything?"

"You didn't forget a thing."

"But nothing happened."

"Oh, but it did. He's pleased. Now, come sit beside me."

Julian obeyed. "What now? How do I speak to him?"

"He'll come to you when he's ready."

Julian fisted his hands and rested them on his knees. "Now I have to wait?"

"There is no need to be in a hurry. He's never early. When the time is right, he'll come. You can't rush these things. What you desire is no small thing. But don't worry. He already knows what you want. He's always listening."

"So there's no ritual you can do to invoke his presence? Or Harold's, for that matter?"

"I told you. Be patient. Relax. Enjoy the rest of your evening. And when you are tired, go to bed."

Julian's finger tapped on his leg. "How's Katy?"

"She's very well. I've encouraged her to embrace the wisdom that comes to her and not fear the darkness when it closes off her mind. She'll be safe. Harold won't hurt her. And through the process, she gains power."

"You're talking about supernatural power?"

"I am."

Julian looked up at the ceiling.

"You don't believe me."

"It's difficult."

She smiled. "You are a man used to relying on his own power. It will take you time."

"I am also a man who enjoys empirical evidence. If supernatural power is true, why don't we see more of it?"

"You will never believe what you refuse to observe. When you first got Eva back, you said yourself that the universe was working in your favor. We've discussed this and yet you continue to resist."

"It's easy to get caught up in the moment. But time strips away the miraculous nature of events. And it is not as though I don't believe to a point. I am here asking for Asmodeus to kill Eva for me. That is not nothing."

"No. But bear in mind that he is subtle. Most of the time. He's not one to show off. He requires a certain amount of faith."

"I believe I have shown that. But you are suggesting that Katy will have powers of her own."

Bea shrugged. "Perhaps you will have to see that to believe it."

"Perhaps I will. But I won't take up any more of

your time tonight."

"You're anxious for a response. Don't be."

"Easier said than done." He stood.

"Sleep well."

"Good night, Bea." He walked toward the door.

"I hope you will consider it."

"Consider what?"

"You could gain powers as well. Would you like that?"

"Who wouldn't?"

"Then simply be open to the possibility."

"I will. I promise. Good night."

Julian retired to his study and started a fire. It wasn't cold enough to warrant one, but he needed the restful environment it would create. Falling asleep wouldn't come easily for him tonight. Even the weariness that had built up behind his eyes wouldn't be enough to overcome his conviction that he shouldn't need any help.

He'd spent so many years convinced of his autonomy as leader in his vision for the future, that trusting in a spiritual being he couldn't fully understand would take time. But he'd put his misgivings aside tonight. He was running out of time to get rid of Eva and receiving help to bring about her death was one thing he wouldn't cower away from.

He sat down with a drink and rested an arm across the back of the couch. The flames licked up the surrounding air, devouring the logs as they intensified.

His focus blurred as he watched, and his eyes drooped. The blaze twisted into shapes that stood out from the rest. Grotesque shapes in human form writhing in agony, just like when he had looked out over the city.

It reminded him of a book he'd read as a young man. Perhaps Dante had seen the same thing before writing *Inferno*. But Julian's dream for the future was not to recreate hell. Perhaps that was part of the reason for resisting Asmodeus. Julian wanted power and control, but only because humanity was not capable of governing itself. Sacrifices were made along the way, but his ultimate goal was utopia, not a netherworld.

"You think our goals are not compatible?" A voice seemed to come from the flames.

Julian wasn't startled by it. He stayed in the half daze as the voice filtered into his mind. "Are you the devil?"

"It matters?"

"If you want a hell on earth. I need you to understand that's not what I want." Julian thought he spoke the words out loud, but they buzzed around in his head and didn't touch his lips.

"That's not true. I want humanity to reach their full potential the same as you. God is the one who does not want humanity to prosper. Why do you think he forbade them to eat the fruit from the tree of knowledge?"

"But they did eat."

"Yes, and God punished them for it, same as he punished me. He could not accept that I was as good as him. He's been keeping us both in bondage ever since. I want to set them free. I want us all to be free."

"Freedom," Julian said. "Yes. Freedom."

"But in order to be free, they must be led."

"Yes. Exactly. That is what I've been trying to do. They are like sheep without a shepherd." *Was that a laugh that came from the flames?* "Do you disagree?"

"No. I completely agree. That is why I need you to lead them where they need to go."

"That is what I'm doing."

"You are making an admirable attempt. But you miss an important part."

"What is that?"

"You need to rise above the humanity you wish to lead. As you are, you do not have the power or the resources needed to complete the course you've set."

"Which is why I've asked for your help."

"But you want to keep me boxed. You would keep me bound the same as God. You want me to do your bidding."

"I—you're right."

"But I am greater than you."

"Yes."

"So allow me to lead you and in turn, you can lead them."

"Yes."

"Good. Time is growing short. You must act and show humanity how vulnerable they are now. A small gesture to begin with. Enough to coax them the way you want. A deed to demonstrate how fragile they are. You must instill fear in order to guide them in the direction they must take."

"What about Eva…and Ben?"

"Let me worry about them. Their greatest weakness is that they don't realize your reach or mine. They believe God is working for them, but God only works for himself."

"But you promised to give her to me."

"And you promised to give yourself to me. Seems neither one of us got what we wanted."

"But I've done it now."

"And now I've found a use for her. When I'm finished, then I will give her to you to do with as you please."

Julian took a sharp intake of breath. "You promise me that?"

"I promise."

Julian snorted awake. He was lying on his side on the couch. The fire still burned strong, and when he looked across the room at the clock, he saw it had only been two minutes since he'd sat down.

He blinked back at the fire, replaying the conversation he'd had. It would have been simple to dismiss it as a dream. Bea had filled his head with strange ideas that could easily manifest as the vision he'd had. But he was done second-guessing. The promise of getting Eva back was too irresistible to reject.

He'd call Michael in the morning and they'd move forward with stage one and Clara could be their first soldier.

Chapter 26

CLARA HUMMED a hymn she'd learned as a girl. The melody filled her mind and formed into words: *When peace like a river attendeth my way...*

Her arms were tied behind her back, and a cut to the inside of her mouth stung but had stopped bleeding.

When sorrows like sea billows roll...

Her shoulder was sore from when Tyler dragged her from the car. But she couldn't blame him entirely. She had resisted, and the old injury from when her late husband threw her across the room had weakened the joint to where it couldn't hold up to maltreatment.

Whatever my lot, Thou has taught me to—Footsteps echoed on the concrete floor and the murmur in her throat choked to a halt.

She didn't recognize the man who entered. He stood before her with his hands on his hips. She guessed he was in his midthirties. He had short-cropped hair and a mean scowl.

"Julian's sent me in here to butter you up."

She didn't mean to laugh, but her dead husband would have been embarrassed to say a ridiculous thing like that. He was always much more straight to the point. Tight-lipped—unless he was cussing at her. In his more lucid moments, he preferred to let his actions speak.

"Butter, huh? You plan on cooking me like a roast? Or are we talking potatoes? Sour cream is always good on potatoes, but I'd recommend getting your hands on some garlic. No need for other seasoning. I'm salty enough."

The man cracked his knuckles. Clara figured it was to buy himself time as he tried to make sense of the crazy woman tied to a chair.

"I'm not a fan of beating up on defenseless old ladies, but you've got to be about the ugliest thing I've ever laid eyes on."

"Ah. That's more like it. I was afraid I'd be stuck in a world of puns and innuendo. My husband was never subtle. I appreciate straight—"

When his fist connected with her face, the inside of her lip split open again. She pressed her tongue to it, using the pain to fan her anger. That was how she had survived in the past, by staying angry. If she allowed the assault to breed despair, she'd be lost.

"Not bad," she said. "But I've had worse."

He grabbed her hair, yanking her head backward. "You don't want me to go easy on you? Fine."

Clara hung in for a while. If it hadn't been for the abuse she'd lived with for so many years, she may have given in to the pain earlier. But she was stubborn and when she finally cried out to God to let her die, she lost consciousness.

A cold shock jerked her awake. The movement sent a blaze of pain through her whole body and she nearly blacked out again. When her mind finally stilled, she found she had water dripping off her head to her shirt that was already soaked.

One good eye blinked toward the floor, where she kept it focused on the feet before her. She pressed a slow breath through her lips to settle the nausea that boiled in her stomach, before lifting her eyes to the man who stood in front of her holding a bucket.

"It is well with my soul," she mumbled through cracked lips.

The man who had beaten her set down the bucket beside the chair and stepped to the side to make room for another man she hadn't seen.

"Julian," Clara said weakly. "You've finally decided to join us."

"Have you been enjoying Salvador's company?"

"Is that his name? You should teach your men manners. He didn't even introduce himself before he beat me. If you're going to touch a lady, you should at least tell her your name. "

Julian looked at Salvador with an eyebrow raised.

"He's good at a lot of things. I'll allow this indiscretion. How are you feeling?"

"Me? Right as rain. But I've had good company."

"I thought you didn't approve of Salvador's manners."

"He's not the one I'm talking about."

"No? Is there someone else here who I missed?"

She saw the quick twitch his eyes made as they darted around the room to confirm no one else was present. He was scared about something.

"I'd tell ya but you'll think I'm crazy." Each word hurt to say, but watching Julian fidget gave her a satisfaction that eased the pain.

"Try me."

God had been whispering in her ear as she was beaten. She couldn't see him, but she was certain he was there. "I wouldn't want to scare you."

"I'm hard to scare."

"I don't think it's as hard as you think."

"Try me."

"I don't know if you're aware of this, but the Lord is working against you. And when the Lord is working against you, you're best to take a step back."

"The *Lord*?" His lips pursed. "I'll take my chances."

The Holy Spirit continued to whisper into her ear. Her eyes lit up. "You believe in supernatural power?"

"If you want to call it that, sure. There's more to the picture than we can see."

"True. But you'd better make sure you're on the right side of the equation. One side is going to lose bad."

"And how do you know it's not you and your *Lord* who is going to lose?"

She shook her head and tsked. "I see."

"What do you see?"

"Who you've put your trust in. It's not ideal to trust the father of lies. But then, you don't really trust him, do you? You only think you have no choice."

He tried to hide the look of shock, but she saw it before he replaced it with a mask of calm. "I take it you believe this banter will buy you time? Do you expect to be rescued? It would certainly make my job easier if Eva turned up."

"I'm safer from you than you realize."

"Perhaps you'll change your opinion if you had another round with Salvador."

"You must have had to scrape the bottom of the barrel to find someone willing to beat up on old ladies. It's despicable, really."

"If I had another way, I would use it. Unfortunately, today, I'll take what I can get."

"That desperate, huh?"

"You're not as innocent as you pretend to be."

"Who said anything about innocent?"

"All right. You've had your fun. Now, unless you want me to leave you with Salvador, tell me what I need to know."

"I'll tell you what you need to know if you answer me one question."

"I can certainly try."

"Is Bigfoot real?"

"Clara, please. You're a better person than this, surely."

"You said you'd answer my question if you could. Does that mean you can't?"

Julian sighed. "Very well. If it gets me what I need— No. Bigfoot is not real."

"Wrong."

"You've seen him?"

"No."

"Okay, Bigfoot is real. Happy?"

"No. That's the wrong answer as well."

"You really are stalling for time."

He spoke quietly into Salvador's ear, then turned his attention back to Clara as the other man left the room. "So there is no right answer to satisfy you?"

"Sure there is. The right answer is 'I don't know.' I've studied conspiracies for a long time and understand that a negative response to something that cannot be proven or disproven necessitates the reality that he does, in fact, exist. And he is quite possibly on your payroll. Why else explicitly deny his existence?"

Julian's smile was close-lipped. Men like him were so easy to irritate.

"Fine. I own Bigfoot. I use him for covert operations."

"I knew it."

"Now tell me what I need to know."

"Okay. You need to accept Jesus Christ as your Lord and savior in order to be free."

He squeezed the bridge of his nose. "I've had a frustrating couple of days. I don't have the patience for your jokes."

"You think I'm joking? You asked me to tell you what you needed to know. That's what you need to know."

"I would also like to know where Eva is and what she's been planning. Has she gotten her memory back? Why did she visit Lyons?"

"I've got no idea what you're talking about. They don't tell me nothin'. Ben thinks I'm a loony, just like you do. He won't trust me with sensitive information like that."

"Eva would have told you something. She must trust you if she sought shelter at your house. Especially after what you did to her."

"She returned to my place because she had no other choice."

Julian took a step closer so he could tower over her. "Tell me where Eva is."

Clara ignored the sting in her lips as they curved into a smile.

"Does that smile indicate you have no intention of answering my question?"

"Ever since you and your thugs turned up at my house and kidnapped me, I have been praying you wouldn't get your hands on Eva or Ben. Looks like my prayers have thwarted your plans. You got guys at my house lying in wait, right?"

"We know she's staying there."

"She was." Clara laughed, then coughed, nearly passing out from the pain. "She would have been back by now." Her ribs burned. "If she's not, then she's long gone."

"She can't evade me forever."

"Sure she can."

"We'll agree to disagree."

"Does that mean you'll let me go now?"

"We're not anywhere close to done with you yet. You've got a lot of spirit, I'll give you that. But it's a spirit I am determined to break." Julian grabbed an ice pick off the table and held it close to Clara's face. "I will do whatever it takes to crack you open."

Clara looked at the weapon. She believed him. But she'd endure for as long as she could. "Okay, I'll tell you. Just, please don't use that thing on me."

Julian stepped back, a smug look on his face. "So?"

"We know what you've been hiding."

"Can you be more specific?"

"The power that you have. The technology. We know where it comes from."

"You think so?"

"We know. Eva and Ben are working right now to destroy the aliens you've been hiding."

Julian closed his eyes. "We're done here."

"You going to give me a lift back to my place, or will I have to call a cab?"

"Information is not the only reason I've brought you here. I have another, more important use for you. But for now, I'll excuse myself. I have some things to set up so you can help the advancement of my foundation."

"Nice try," Clara yelled as he walked out the door. "You'll never get me to help you with nothin'."

Her body sagged once the door was closed. She was a stubborn old woman who had been unwilling to show Julian how weak she was, but it took everything she had to hold out as long as she did. Her head hung in exhaustion.

She didn't have the strength to hum, but the words still filled her thoughts and gave her soul strength.

The trump shall resound, and the Lord shall descend. Even so, it is well with my soul...

Chapter 27

WHEN BEN'S EYES OPENED, he didn't move. His muscles tensed as his senses strove to identify where he was.

Then he remembered. The motel.

The man at the desk hadn't asked questions when they gave him their names. He just showed them to a room at the end of a row. It had an extra window and would have been the one Ben would choose if he'd had the option. The window had a clear view of the parking lot and a quick escape out the back, if needed.

He tilted his head sideways and looked at the other bed, where Eva was still asleep. If circumstances had been different, he would have insisted on separate rooms, but he'd slept better knowing she was right there.

Slipping silently out of bed, he headed for a shower. He prayed again for Clara's safety. He and Eva had both fallen asleep praying. But as he closed the door to the bathroom, he stopped. Safety wasn't what she needed prayer for right now. There was another more pressing need.

Wisdom? He said the word to see if it triggered anything as he stood underneath the hot water.

Wisdom was certainly valuable. He added God's wisdom to his prayer, but that wasn't it either.

Should I pray against fear? Hopelessness? Peace?

He tried different words, but nothing was right. He had to stop striving and keep his payer simple.

Lord, you know what she needs. Be by her side. Speak to her. Let her know you're there. Help her to…

Forgiveness. The word formed in his mind and he nearly brushed it away.

"Forgiveness? Is that what she needs?" He knew what Julian was capable of and what he would likely do to Clara. If she survived, she'd need to find a way to forgive him, but that wasn't it.

Forgiveness was right, but the "who" was still a vague perception. He didn't really need to know who.

Whatever and whoever she needs to forgive, Holy Spirit, give her the strength to do it.

When he came out of the bathroom, Eva was on the phone. She nodded acknowledgment to Ben.

"You're certain all three are voting against it?" She listened. "Great. Get onto the others and I'll let you know how we go."

She hung up. "Morning."

"Morning."

"Did you sleep?"

"Yeah, you?"

"I must have."

"That was Lynn?"

"Yeah. She said she's got three more."

He dropped onto the bed, bouncing a little. "That's great."

"Several she spoke to said they were originally for the bill but had changed their minds."

Ben nodded. "God's in this."

"Yeah. We still have a lot of ground to cover and not much time to do it, but God's already doing his part. Now we need to do ours—What's wrong?"

"Clara. I know we need to trust God with her, too, but I hate that Julian's got her."

"I know. We should never have left her."

"We couldn't have known. We know what God can do with every move we make, even when it looks wrong."

"That doesn't make it any easier."

"No. But all we can do right now is keep praying for her, and keep taking one step at a time. I've been thinking we should go speak to Rodriguez, like you suggested."

Eva shook her head. "Rodriguez can wait. Lynn said we should pay Hoak a visit."

"Why Hoak? Do you know him?"

"I know of him. He's not loyal to Julian and Lynn thinks if we get him on our side, he'll convince others. But he's…old-fashioned."

"What does that mean?"

"He'll respond better if a man speaks to him. And he was in the armed forces, so you can work your connection there as well. He'll respect you."

Ben pinched his lips together before responding. "Old-fashioned, huh?"

"If he needs to speak to a man, he can speak to a man. I don't care as long as the bill doesn't get through."

"Then let's go have a chat with Hoak."

Eva had to employ her old skills in manipulation in order to get an urgent meeting with Donald Hoak, appealing to his pride.

"I must say, I was surprised," the senator said as he ushered Sergeant Benjamin Waite and his personal assistant into his office. "I haven't had a great deal to do with the special forces in recent years."

"You may not have been paying attention to us, but we've been watching you for some time."

Hoak laughed. "I don't know whether I should take that as a compliment or a threat."

"It's a great compliment, I assure you. I appreciate your willingness to see me on such short notice," Ben said as he sat.

"I'll be truthful with you. I've never heard of the award you want to present me with. Can you run me through it? Is it unusual to have a preliminary meeting about these things?"

"It is unusual, yes. But there are some important items we need to discuss beforehand." Ben looked back at Eva, who had remained by the door to make sure they had no interruptions.

"Fire away." Hoak sat in his wide leather chair and leaned back like he had all the time in the world.

"This upcoming bill regarding privacy. You will vote in favor of it?"

Hoak's chair tilted forward and the smile on his face drifted into unease. "What does my vote have to do with the award?"

"Nothing, I'm afraid. There is no award."

"I'm not following."

"We're not here about an award," Eva said.

"We're here because Julian Underwood needs to be stopped," Ben finished.

Hoak's face paled, then reddened. His voice was low and gruff. "Please leave my office immediately."

"We aren't here to hurt you. We just want to talk."

Hoak picked up his phone, so Ben pulled out his weapon. "Please put that down. I told you, we just want to talk."

"How did you get a weapon in here?"

"It wasn't easy. But it's important that you hear us out."

"Who are you?"

"Ben Waite. I was in the special forces, but I am not involved with them now. I used to work for the Underwood Foundation, and we know Julian is determined to see this bill pass, but we can't let that happen."

"Let me get this straight. You believe the bill will give the Underwood Foundation power it shouldn't have?"

"We know it will. That's why we're here. We need to

stop him from gaining more control than he already has. Stopping that bill would make our job much easier."

"Sir," Eva said. "It's imperative that the bill doesn't pass."

Ben gave her a warning look. "It will give Julian unprecedented access to the lives of American citizens."

"That's ridiculous. Who told you that? This bill is about saving millions of lives in a worst-case scenario."

"No." Eva took a step forward. "It will destroy millions of lives."

"And who are you exactly? Not Ben's personal assistant, I take it?"

"My name is Eva Underwood. I'm Julian's daughter." The word was bitter in her mouth, but she needed to prove her authority on the matter.

"Ah, yes. I hadn't taken any notice, but I recognize you now. You were missing not long ago? I thought Julian was the one who rescued you, and now you're turning against him?"

"Julian is a monster and yes, I will do everything in my power to stop him."

"What you're suggesting is preposterous. There will be safeguards in place. Julian would never have the access you presume he will. It's just not possible."

"I spent a lot of years under Julian's spell. I know what he's capable of, and I know what he's planning. He's already secured the contract to create the hub for the collection of data."

"That's impossible. They wouldn't give that out to a private contractor, and not before the bill has been passed."

"Not officially, but he has the right people in play to make it happen almost immediately."

"I'm sorry, but I can't be a part of this. I'll vote the way my conscience dictates."

"Your conscience?" Eva scoffed. "Are you kidding me?"

How could they ever change Hoak's mind short of threatening to end his life?

"We're risking our lives to come here," Ben said.

Hoak shook his head. "I'm sorry. I can't help you." He attempted a look of disdain, but his eyes carried another emotion.

"Senator," Eva said. "We know this has nothing to do with your conscience. If you don't rise above yourself and do what you know to be right—"

"What I know to be right? You walk into my office on false pretenses and then point a gun in my face to force me to do what you want. You're as bad as Julian."

"So you admit Julian is not a good person."

Hoak paled. "He's got nothing to do with this."

"He's found something out, hasn't he? He's got something on you now."

"I don't know what you're talking about. I make my own decisions." He shuffled papers around on his desk, avoiding eye contact with either of them.

Eva squinted. There was something about him. It wasn't just the fear; it was the conflict. Then she knew. She didn't know how, but it was suddenly clear.

"You're a Christian."

Hoak's head snapped her way. "What? No, I—" His eyes dropped to the floor. "How did you know that?"

"Was it a secret?" Ben asked.

"It's private."

"Oh, I see," Eva said. "You want to be a Christian, but you don't want it to cost you anything."

"I don't think it's any of your business."

"Does that help you sleep—"

"Eva," Ben said.

She crossed her arms and turned her body to take herself out of the conversation while she calmed down. Ben was right to stop her. She wasn't helping the situation by making it more emotional.

"Senator Hoak," Ben said. "Eva and I are Christians."

"Is that why you think your way is right? What if my way is?"

Eva clenched her teeth to keep from responding.

"That may be," Ben said. "But can I ask what the real reason is for your vote? Eva believes that Julian knows something about you. If that's not the case, if it really is your conscience that urges you to vote yes, then fine. We'll leave you alone."

"You will?"

"Yes. But if it's something else—if it's Julian—all I ask is that you don't forget that God is the only one who matters here. I don't care if your faith is private, but if you truly believe in a God who would give the life of his son for humanity, then you need to forget about Julian's threats and ask God what he really wants you to do. You're in a profession where you can influence the laws of the land. That is a powerful position and carries a great weight of responsibility. All we want is for you to ask yourself honestly if being a part of Julian's plan is the right thing to do."

Hoak's face distorted in indecision. "Of course it's not the right thing to do."

"There's still time to change your vote."

"If Julian reveals my secrets, I won't be able to keep my job."

"You think you'll be able to live with yourself if you're part of helping Julian? It's not worth it."

Hoak turned in his seat to look out the window. "Why did you come here?" he mumbled. "For years I prided myself that I had no skeletons in the closet. Then I made one mistake, and it cost me everything. I've had to lie to myself every day to get the job done and then you walk in here and change everything. "

"We didn't change anything. We just brought it out into the open. It would have destroyed you in the end."

"Can you let me think about it?"

"I'm sorry, but we're running out of time. We need to know if you're with us, and if so, is there anyone else you have an influence on that you can turn?"

Hoak sighed, then swiveled back around in his seat. He looked at Eva first, then at Ben. "You're asking me to make a life-altering decision in a matter of minutes."

"Only because you followed Julian's orders in the first place." Eva pressed her lips together when Ben caught her eye. "I'm sorry. I, of all people, know how controlling he can be." She took a deep breath. "Senator, I know how hard this is. I'm sorry it's come to this, but this is too important to leave alone. Julian has a large majority. We need to turn every vote we can."

"Have you turned anyone else yet?"

"Yes," Ben said.

"Is it going to be enough?"

"We don't know," Eva said.

"I'll give you my answer if you give me a truthful answer to my question."

"We'll try."

"Lyons's death. Was that really a home invasion like they're saying? Or was that Julian?"

Ben looked at Eva, who shrugged.

"It was Julian," Ben said.

"So it's not simply ruin I'm facing. It's death."

"Either that, or the fall of the country. It's your choice."

Hoak squeezed his eyes closed. "Fine. I'll do it."

Eva sagged against the wall.

"Is there anyone else who you believe you could turn?" Ben said.

"Franklin's not in Julian's pocket. I know that for sure. I'll explain to him what's going on behind the scenes and he'll turn. There are a few more I can speak to."

"Thank you."

Chapter 28

CLARA WAS WEAK. They hadn't given her anything to eat or drink and her body wasn't strong enough to recover from the damage like it used to be.

"It's okay if you take me now," she whispered to God. "I'm ready to go."

The door opened and she lifted her head. An older woman she hadn't seen before walked in and shut the door gently.

The newcomer studied Clara for a moment with a deep frown that pushed a crease between her eyes. "Clara, my name is Bea." She shook her head and sighed. "They haven't been very nice to you, have they? We'll have to change that."

"You must—" The words caught in Clara's dry throat.

"Wait a moment. Don't speak yet." Bea put a bag on the nearby table and pulled out a bottle of water. She held it to Clara's lips and let her drink as much as she could. "Is that better?"

"It would be better if I wasn't tied up."

"Yes, I'm sorry about that. I would untie you, but Julian refuses while I'm alone with you. He's concerned for my safety."

"Smart man. You should be. I think my arm might be broken, but I'd still have a go at you if I could. No offense."

"None taken." She took her time putting the bottle back in the bag before pulling a chair close. "I don't blame you for being angry. Anyone would be in your position, but I want you to know that I'm here as a friend."

"Sure you are."

"You don't believe me? No, of course you wouldn't. I wouldn't, either, if I were in your position."

"I'd be happy to trade." She tried to make her lips smile, but it hurt too much.

"Julian didn't want me to visit with you. I don't know what he's afraid of, but it was important that I come."

"Why?"

"I'm here because I received a message for you."

Clara closed her one good eye. Being obstinate drained her energy. "From who?"

"Simon."

"Simon who?"

"Your husband."

She couldn't believe that the sound of his name could still put a knot in her stomach. "I don't know who you think you spoke to, but Simon's dead. Blew himself to smithereens years ago."

"I know. He told me."

Clara found it hard to hold her head up, but when she heard that, she had to look the woman in the eye. "He told you?"

"I have a gift for speaking to the dead."

"Speaking to the dead is the devil's work."

"I'm sorry you think so."

Clara let her head drop. "It doesn't matter. I'm not interested in hearing what he has to say, anyway."

"Are you sure? You might be surprised."

"Doubt it."

"He says he's sorry."

Clara let a laugh slip out before she could stop it and a tear escaped from the pain. It took several breaths before she could respond. "Now I know it ain't Simon you've been talking to. 'Sorry' did not exist in his vocabulary."

"I'm sure it didn't while he was on the earth. But he's been suffering. He's been paying the penalty for the way he treated you."

"What's that mean?"

"Let's just say, he now knows how it felt to be you."

Clara had spent a lot of years wishing Simon knew what she'd endured at his hand. She'd always said she'd forgiven him, knowing deep down it wasn't true. But if he understood how she'd suffered, maybe she could finally find the power to do it.

"You're saying he's in hell being beaten up?"

"He's in agony for all eternity. He wants you to forgive him."

"Would his pain stop if I do?"

"No. But perhaps it could help him endure."

She hated him, but imagining him in pain for all of eternity didn't make her feel good either. "Well then, tell him I forgave him a long time ago."

"That's kind of you. I knew you were a good woman as soon as I saw you."

"Does that mean Julian will let me go?"

Bea smiled sadly. "I'm here on my own, not for Julian. If I had things my way…but there's no point thinking like that. It's not the way things are."

"So that's all you came for? As a messenger for my late husband?"

"Yes, but there's more."

Clara tsked. "I knew it. Whenever Simon showed an ounce of decency, it was always 'cause he wanted somethin'. So what is it?"

"Don't underestimate the power that death has on a person. If you could see him, you'd know how remorseful he truly is."

"Sure he is. So what else did he bring up?"

"He mentioned Franky."

"Franky's in prison."

"I know."

"Does he?"

"Yes. He was concerned because of what Franky was arrested for."

"He was going to blow things up. He had an arsenal and he had plans."

"Yes. I did see that on the news."

"Don't tell me Simon thinks he's innocent. I know my son. I know he did, in fact, want to blow things up."

"Yes, but you don't know why."

"What difference does it make?"

"It makes a difference because the FBI arrested him because he was trying to destroy an illegal operation they've been running."

"What? How do you know that?"

"The dead can see many things. The spirit realm removes many barriers."

"And how do I know I can believe you?"

"Because you understand things in a way many others don't. They call you a conspiracy nut, but you know that is only because you're getting too close to the truth and they need to discredit you. Why do you think the FBI turned up at your house in the first place?"

"Because we had Eva."

"The FBI took over that investigation. Why? After Eva was safe, they still went into your house and searched it. Why would they need to do that? You know how they work. I don't need to spell it out for you."

"Okay, let's say I believe you. So what?"

"I know you don't like Julian, but—"

"That's a mild word for it."

"Obviously he hasn't treated you in a way to make you feel otherwise. However, as it turns out, you two have a common enemy."

"Is that so? I guess we should paint each other's nails and have a slumber party."

"Franky knew what the FBI was doing and he wanted to stop them. He was going to destroy their operation."

"And?"

"Clara, Franky is innocent. If he'd accomplished his

plan, he would have exposed what the FBI was doing. He would have been a hero. There are those very high up in the Bureau who would have gone to prison for a very long time."

"You talk about him like he's a saint."

"I expected you to think more highly of your own son."

"You can paint whatever picture you want of Franky, but I know him. He deserves to be in prison. It's safer for everyone if he's locked up."

"But that's not where it ends. Like I said, Simon knows more than we can. What he's discovered is that they don't want Franky to go to prison. In prison, he can still talk. They don't want him to have the opportunity to tell anyone what he was doing."

"What are you saying?"

"The FBI is plotting to murder your son to keep him quiet."

Clara's mind was clouded by the pain. She knew she couldn't trust Bea, but her fear for her son closed off a concern for anything else. She knew he should pay for the wrongs he did, but she didn't want her son to die. Especially if what Bea said was true. And she wanted so desperately to believe that Franky had some good left in him. That he wanted to protect people. That he could be a hero.

"What am I supposed to do when I'm tied up in here? Even if I was out there, there's nothing I could do."

"But there is. You can finish what Franky started."

"How?"

"By destroying the FBI's operation and exposing the truth. You do that and Julian will make sure that Franky is exonerated."

"He can do that?"

"You might not like him, but even you have to admit he has a lot of influence. I can guarantee Franky will be protected."

"But why would Julian want to help me?"

"I told you, you have a common enemy."

"So I'd be helping Julian."

"In exchange for your son's life. If you ask me, you're getting more out of this deal than anyone. What is more important than the life of a child?"

"I don't know. I don't know how I can be a part of helping Julian."

"I know you don't agree with his ethos, but focus on your son. You have the chance to save him. What mother would give up that opportunity? It was the last thing Simon said to me. He pleaded with me to tell you because he knows how much you love Franky. He knows how much you've already sacrificed for him, and he knows you are the only one in the world who would help. Clara, you are Franky's only hope."

Clara imagined Franky, not as the angry man she saw last, but the carefree boy who tried to protect her when Simon attacked. It wasn't his fault he turned out the way he did. She really was his only hope. "How—how can I be sure you're even telling the truth?"

"Unfortunately, you can't. I can give you nothing but my word. But I swear to you on the god that you serve, that I am not lying."

"He could strike you dead if you are."

Bea looked up at the ceiling and smiled. "And yet here I am, still alive."

"What if I say no?"

"Then Julian will kill you. He'll still get what he wants, but you'll die and so will your son. I'm sorry. I wish I could change his mind, but I don't have that kind of influence over him. If you want to save Franky, this is your only way. Please. You have nothing to lose and everything to gain."

Clara closed her eyes and tried to pray, but all she could see was Franky, who was trying to do the right thing for once in his life.

"What do I need to do?"

———

Clara hobbled along the sidewalk. They'd cleaned the blood off her, but dressed her up in rags. She was too damaged to send out in public any other way. No one would bother to look at a broken old homeless woman. No one would question her bruised and swollen face.

She clutched her arm against her chest. There would be ligaments torn from her shoulder, but she was astonished to learn that she had no broken bones. At least, that's what the doctor said who assessed her. But she didn't trust anyone who could see she was being abused and look the other way.

She stopped moving when a kid came running toward her. He was looking at his phone and for a moment, she was sure they would collide. But at the last second he saw her and sidestepped, scowling like the near impact was her fault.

It took her a full minute to move again. She'd flinched at the near miss and now paid for it. But none of the pain constricting her breathing would matter soon. She only had to endure a little longer, then it would all be over.

She studied the ground in front of her to ensure each step would go unhindered. Then she heard a laugh, and she looked up to see a woman with her arm slipped through the arm of her companion. She was laughing at something he'd said. He grinned, appreciating her enjoyment. To her right, a man was leaning against a wall, lighting a cigarette.

Normal life surrounded her. A life she'd never known and never wanted. Perhaps it was better not to think too deeply about what was really going on in the world. Did it make for a satisfying life to be unaware that an old homeless woman was about to set off an explosion that would kill people? Soon they'd all be glued to their TVs and phones to get the latest on the bombing but remain unaffected by it in any meaningful way.

She dropped her gaze back to the ground. The painkillers they'd given to her so she could function left a heavy cloud hanging over her head, but it couldn't completely remove the nagging thought that kept scratching at the back of her mind. She tried to blink it away and focus on the trigger her hand was wrapped around in her pocket. That trigger meant Franky's freedom. She had to focus on Franky's freedom.

But Simon's confession of remorse was also tugging at her thoughts. She wasn't surprised he was in hell being tortured. He always said he was a God-fearing man, but that had never registered for her. She couldn't reconcile it. And the thought of meeting him one day in heaven was sickening. But maybe she wasn't destined for heaven either. She'd said she'd forgiven him, but she knew that wasn't true. She'd spent her adult life telling Simon the things he wanted to hear, and she still did, even now. Even in death he controlled her and she knew why.

Somehow through the fog, each thump of her foot on the pavement drew her closer to the revelation that forgiving him was the only way she could be free from him. Whether he was truly sorry for what he'd done or not, whether or not he deserved it, she had to find a way to forgive him.

Most people didn't know when their lives would end, but she did. It was a gift knowing that today would be her last day on earth, and she wouldn't waste it. She'd go. But she'd go free.

When she stopped walking again, she scanned the buildings nearby. Julian would be watching, but if he wanted her cooperation, he'd have to wait.

"Jesus," she said out loud. A woman walking past dropped her head toward the ground and took a wider berth to get around her.

She didn't care. She was ready. "Jesus, I forgive him. You forgave me for all the horrible things I've done. I don't have a right to hold him accountable because you no longer hold me accountable. You do as you see fit to him. I won't take responsibility for that anymore. If he stands in judgment, it will be to you, the only righteous judge, not me."

If he was going to suffer in hell, she wouldn't have that on her hands.

A weight in her chest lifted, and a smile lit her face. It felt as though she'd been breathing through a straw her whole life and had only now taken her first full breath.

Lifting her face to the heavens, the warmth of the sun touched her blotchy broken skin, even with heavy clouds filling the sky. Joy filled her chest and she looked around the street for someone to celebrate with. Everyone avoided eye contact, or stared—if they were brazen enough. She didn't care. If everyone thought she was crazy, fine. This was the best kind of crazy she'd ever felt.

She limped along again at a faster pace, not fully aware of where she was going until she found herself in front of the hospital.

The smile dropped from her face. This was where Bea said the FBI was running their operation. To the public, the east wing was full of cancer patients, but that was the front. That's what Bea said.

She squeezed her arm tighter to her chest as she walked inside. She'd made the decision to follow through on this, but even the painkillers couldn't keep her concern at bay any longer. Despite the medication, her mind was clearer than it had been in decades.

She looked around the waiting room and froze. What was she doing here? Why had she agreed to this?

Eva and Ben had stopped Julian from blowing up a library with kids in it. Here she was about to blow up cancer patients if what Bea had said was a lie.

"No. No, I can't."

She had been so consumed with Simon and Franky in the fog of the pain and drugs that she'd been convinced of what Bea had told her. She'd been momentarily brainwashed and she should have known better. Bea couldn't speak to the dead. She was lying or she was working with the devil.

A police officer was speaking to a nurse across the room. Clara hurried over to him. "You need to help me."

The officer turned to her, igniting a spark of fear. She didn't trust the police. What if they arrested her and blamed her for everything? Or what if Bea hadn't been lying and Franky was going to be killed by the FBI?

"Ma'am, are you okay?"

"I—" She had to do this. She wouldn't put her life or Franky's life into Julian's hand. She wouldn't allow Simon—or something pretending to be him—control her.

"I belong to God."

"Pardon me?" The officer said, tensing.

"I'm sorry."

She pulled open her coat a little to expose the bomb they'd strapped to her. "Please. I need your help. They want me to blow up the hospital."

Chapter 29

"I THINK WE MIGHT DO THIS," Eva said when they got back to the truck.

"Yeah. It's looking good. But we shouldn't be surprised. God's in this. We've seen it the whole time."

Eva leaned her head back on the seat, and Ben turned on the radio. He flipped through the stations until he found a song he knew and they headed back to the motel.

"Do you think Clara's okay?" Eva said when the song finished.

"I have no idea. I just keep praying that God will keep her safe, but I don't know. We both know Julian."

"I hate this. I've lived with horrors my whole life. It was easier when I didn't care."

"But that's no way to live."

"No, it's not."

"We've had breaking news…"

The DJ's words caught Ben's attention, and he

turned up the volume. Anything breaking these days could be connected to Julian.

"Reports have begun pouring in that there has been an explosion at Methodist General Hospital. At this time, we have no further details, but we will keep you updated as we find out more."

Ben and Eva looked at each other. "Clara," they both said and Ben turned the truck around.

"God, please don't let it be Clara. Please," Eva prayed. "Not like that." She pressed her hand to her face when she couldn't stop the tears. "Please."

Ben blew tight breaths out between his lips in an attempt to ease his anger. He should have killed Julian when he had the chance.

God, why let Julian do that to her? You saved my life, but not hers? It didn't matter that he didn't know any details. He knew. After Julian tried to blow up a library, a hospital would be a reasonable next step for him. Involving Clara would have been icing on the cake for him.

"She's dead." Eva said, wiping the tears from her cheek.

"We don't know that yet."

"But I know Julian better than anyone else…" Eva closed her eyes. "I can't. I can't think about it."

"We'll get down there and see what we can find out."

The scene when Ben and Eva arrived at the hospital was chaos. They had to park blocks away and even then, the police line wouldn't let them get close. But they were close enough to view the gaping hole where the emergency department used to be.

Ben pushed through the horde to the police officers who were keeping the crowd back. "Excuse me, Officer."

"I'm sorry, sir. We are unable to answer any of your questions," one of the officers said.

Eva stepped forward. "We had a family member inside."

"I'm sorry, ma'am. They're evacuating the hospital to all nearby medical facilities. I can give you a number you can call to get details of your relative's transfer if you like."

Her shoulders fell. "Yeah, thanks." She numbly wrote the number on her hand, then she and Ben moved away from the line. "We'll never find her. If she was involved in the explosion, there would be nothing left. I don't know why we came here."

"We don't know that she died," Ben said, leading her back to the truck.

Eva yanked out of his grip. "Of course we do. She's dead, Ben. We have to accept that. We always knew there would be sacrifices."

"Clara would never have voluntarily participated. I'm not ready to give up hope."

"Then what do you suggest we do?"

"Call the number the cop gave you and give them a description of Clara. We'll say she went to the emergency room, but may not have checked in yet."

"But if she was wearing a vest like the guy in the library—"

"Then they won't have anyone matching that description." Ben's voice was barely above a whisper. "We have nothing to lose."

Eva stared at the phone in her hand.

"You want me to do it?" Ben said.

She handed him the phone, and he made the call. A recorded message came up that the lines were all busy and they should try later.

"Busy. We'll have to wait."

"I'm no good at waiting."

"Me either."

"So what do we do?"

He tapped his finger on the steering wheel. "Is there anyone else we can talk to about the bill?"

"No, it's up to Lynn and the guys she has working with her. They know how to talk the talk better than we do and she hasn't got anyone worth me following up."

"I'll go crazy if I don't do anything."

"If I was on my own, I'd go for a run. A hard one."

"Then let's do that."

Eva nodded. "I know a place."

When they arrived back at the motel, they were both exhausted. Ben was glad for it because he had a deep ache in his chest that made it tempting to draw close to Eva. But he wouldn't risk that.

He fell onto his bed and turned away from her. The

enormity of everything they faced weighed heavily on them both. He was confident they'd get enough votes tomorrow to stop the bill, but that wouldn't put an end to Julian's work. It was only one step. They'd still have to find out what he planned next, and with Clara's death looming, it felt like an impossible task to ultimately stop the man. They couldn't go on like this forever.

"Should we try again?" Eva said.

Ben rolled over to look at her. She was sitting on the edge of her bed with the phone in her hand.

"Sure."

She put the phone to her ear and waited, then hung it up. "Still no luck."

"We should get some rest." He wanted to reach out to her, so he rolled back over and pulled the blanket across his legs, falling into an uneasy sleep.

Eva woke early feeling anxious. It looked like Ben hadn't moved all night. She focused on his back, looking for his breathing. The last thing she should worry about was Ben dying in his sleep, but she trusted very few people, and with the possibility that they'd lost Clara, she couldn't bear the thought of doing this without him.

She watched him sleep for another minute. His even breaths suggested he was asleep.

She slipped out of bed and crept outside to call Lynn.

"I'm sorry if I woke you," she said when Lynn's answer was groggy.

"No. I haven't been sleeping much. I don't imagine either of you have either."

"No. Not really. How's it going on your end?"

"I wasn't confident we'd make it at first, but it looks like we've done it. I don't think we'll win by a landslide, but with the work you and Ben did, we've been able to cover more ground than I expected to. A lot of people have been very receptive."

"Despite my lack of faith. I don't know why I find it so hard to believe that God can do miracles."

"Because you're human. I don't think any of us have gotten through this without doubts licking at our heels. But we've kept moving forward and now we get to see the victory."

"I feel awful that Marcus was killed."

"Yeah. Lyons would have been a great asset into the future. He had a lot of influence. But the bottom line is, we can't trust in man. God's done this. Now we just wait and watch."

"Then we have to figure out the next step."

"And we will."

"I guess." Eva's voice quavered.

"What is it? Has something happened you're not telling me?"

"I didn't want to upset you. You needed to focus."

"Eva, what is it?"

"It's Clara. Julian got to her."

"No. I'm so sorry."

"Did you hear about the hospital explosion?"

"Don't tell me. Right now, the media are reporting the possibility of a terrorist attack."

"It has to be Julian. And we think he may have used Clara."

"But why would Clara agree to that?"

"He didn't have to give her a choice. It's the sort of thing Julian would do."

"Does that mean—she didn't make it?"

"We don't know."

"But you're holding on to hope."

"I don't know which is worse, hanging on to an impossibility only to put off the inevitable, or accepting it. I always thought I would be one hundred percent in this. All the way to the end. I wanted to stop Julian or die trying, but my heart feels like it's being broken over and over again and I don't know how much of it I can take."

"I wish winning with this bill meant it was over, but we'll only slow him down."

Eva squeezed her forehead. "Listen, once we confirm about Clara, we might come your way and get everyone together who's on our side. We need to regroup."

"Yeah. I can find a place to keep you guys safe. I've gotta get going. I've got a lot to do this morning. Keep me posted."

After hanging up, Eva tried the number the officer gave her again. This time the call connected.

Ben blinked awake. A small amount of light filtered in through the window. He rolled onto his back and checked Eva's bed. It was empty. He could hear the quiet tone of her voice outside the door.

This was the day they'd been working toward, and even though he reminded himself that God was bigger than all of this, it still felt like the fate of humanity rested on this moment.

He pressed the heel of his hand into his eye to rub the sleep away when the door flew open. Eva stood, shadowed in the door by the light outside. "I think I found her."

Ben shot up. "Clara?"

"Yeah. I think she's alive."

Ben jumped out of bed, grabbing his shirt and tugging it over his head. "What did they say?"

"I gave them a description, and they said they had an unidentified woman fitting it. She's in bad shape, but she's alive."

"Then let's go."

Eva's heart was racing when they entered the hospital. She cracked her knuckles, then kept squeezing her fingers while they waited to speak to the man at the desk.

He hung up the phone and gave them his attention. "Can I help you?"

"Yes," Eva said. "We believe my mother was in that blast yesterday. When I rang the number to check, they said a woman was brought in who fit her description.

They didn't have her name in the system, so I don't think she had a chance to check in."

"Name?"

"Clara Palmer. But like I said, they didn't have her name. She's an older woman. Heavyset."

"Okay. Give me a moment."

The man made a call. He explained the situation, then frowned and hung up. "If you'd like to have a seat, the doctor will be out shortly to speak to you."

"Is she okay? Is she still alive?"

"Like I said. If you'll sit down, the doctor will be out soon."

Ben took her arm and gently pulled her toward the chairs. "He can't tell us anything. Come and sit down."

Eva's jiggling leg shook the connected row of seats. "I don't want her to be dead. I knew the cost of this going in, but I don't want to lose her. I really don't."

"I know." He put a hand on her knee to settle the bounce. "The doctor will be out soon."

It was another fifteen minutes before a man in scrubs came through the door. He spoke to the man at the desk, who indicated their way.

Eva stood before he reached them. "How is she? Is she alive?"

"My name is Dr. Murphy. You believe your mother is our Jane Doe?"

"Her name is Clara. I'm her daughter, Eva. Is she okay?"

"The woman we have is alive, yes, but she was very close to the blast when it happened. She's already had several surgeries, and she's in the ICU now. The next twenty-four hours are crucial."

"Can we see her?" Ben asked.

"I'll need you to identify if she is your mother, yes. But you can't stay with her for long. She's due for more surgeries."

"Then let's go," Eva said.

"I have to warn you, she's suffered injuries over most of her body. You may find it distressing."

"We understand."

The doctor looked at Ben. "Only family members can come through at this time. Is he your husband?"

"Uh, yes. He is. He's family. Please, can we see her?"

Dr. Murphy nodded, then led them down several corridors and up an elevator to a room that had too much space.

When Eva saw the woman on the bed, her body broken and full of tubing, she closed her eyes for a moment to steady herself.

Ben put a hand on her back. "That's her," he said to the doctor. "That's Clara Palmer."

Eva held her breath as she walked up to the bed. She wanted to wrap Clara in bubble wrap and keep her safe. She looked exposed and vulnerable lying there.

She looked at the doctor. "Can we have a minute?"

"Of course. I'll add her name to the paperwork and we'll get more details from you later."

Eva nodded, but kept her focus on Clara.

Ben stood next to her. "You okay?"

"I've seen this all before, but seeing it happen to someone you care about feels like my insides are being shredded. I know how to torture people, but this has to be the worst form of torture."

Ben reached forward and rested a hand on Clara's leg. He whispered a word of prayer that Eva couldn't hear, but guessed he was praying for healing. She closed her eyes and added her own.

Chapter 30

"EXCUSE ME," Dr. Murphy said from the door when he returned. "We need to get her ready for surgery. If you two would like to wait in the waiting room down the hall, I'll come out and speak to you once I know more."

"Thank you," Eva said, allowing Ben to usher her out of the room. They made their way down the hall and found the small waiting room empty.

"So now we're supposed to sit in the waiting room and wait?"

"That's all we would have been doing back at the motel." He checked the time. "We can check the news. They'll have the results of the bill shortly."

"After seeing Clara like that, I don't even care. I know it still matters, but all I want is for Clara to be okay. I don't think I've ever felt so helpless."

"I know. But wouldn't it be nice to give her the good news about the bill once she wakes up? She'll be thrilled and we could all use something to celebrate."

"This would be easier if we had a smartphone from this era so we could use it to get on the internet."

"We'll have to do it the old-fashioned way." Ben turned on the television and found a news station. It was covering the hospital explosion and reporting that police haven't ruled out a terrorist attack yet, although no groups had stepped forward to claim responsibility.

They sat next to each other on a worn couch. Both were sitting at attention.

"We now take you to the White House, where Brian Trainer is standing by with the results from the vote on the privacy bill."

They stood.

"I don't know why I'm nervous," Eva said, rubbing her hands together.

"Thanks, Karen. The entire country has been watching with bated breath as a bill that would give unprecedented access to citizens' private lives has just been voted on. While small-scale protests have marred some major cities, the majority of the public has been behind it, believing that extreme cases call for extreme measures. One man had this to say—"

The screen cut to a man with a kid on his hip. He was speaking to a reporter. "Under normal circumstances, of course, everyone should have privacy, but we are talking about losing our freedom, and I, for one, don't have anything to hide. So if the government needs to have access to our privacy in order to make this country safe, then I am all for that. The only ones opposed must have some serious skeletons in their closets."

The camera cut back to Brian. "The president has already stated that he would support the bill if it passes —" Brian pressed his hand to his ear. "Hold that thought. We've received word and can now confirm the result of the vote. Early reports suggest that it was a landslide vote in favor of the bill. The privacy bill has passed."

"What?" Eva said, stepping closer to the TV as though she could force it to take back the lie. "That's impossible. How could that happen? That's not right."

Ben shook his head slowly, then stepped back and sat. "I don't believe it."

Eva turned. "That can't be true, can it? It can't be. Lynn said we had more than enough."

"Not everyone accepts God's call."

"But we had the votes."

The phone rang in Eva's pocket. "Lynn, how did that happen? And by a large margin? I don't understand."

"That's what they're feeding to the media, but it only just slipped by."

"Why would they bother lying? It doesn't change the results."

"They want people to think that everyone supports it. Make it look like the popular thing. Make those who oppose it believe they are the silent minority. But listen, Eva. I need you and Ben to pray for me."

"Why? What's going on?"

"I knew as soon as the results came in that I was in trouble. We should have won. We had more than enough."

"That's what I thought."

"That means there are a lot I spoke to who told me they'd changed sides, but they voted for Julian in the end. I have to get out of there. Julian will know by now that I worked against him."

"Do you have somewhere safe to go? Where are you now?"

"In my car, but I've got a tail."

"What?"

"I'm being followed."

"Where are you? We'll come to you."

"No. It's too dangerous. Listen, you and Ben pray for me. I'm going to destroy this phone so they can't trace it back to you."

"No, Lynn, wait. Let us help you."

"There's nothing you can do now. If I can ditch the tail, I've got somewhere to go."

"Where?"

"I won't tell you. I don't want you coming to me."

"Then how will we find you?"

"You won't. If I make it out of this alive, I'll find you."

"Lynn."

"Eva, I knew the risks going in. I'm prepared."

"No. You don't know what they could do to you. If Julian gets you—"

"Stop. Just pray."

"Lynn. No."

"Goodbye, Eva."

To be continued…

Enjoy the book?

Book reviews are the most powerful tool I have as an author to grow my readership. If I had the sway of a New York publisher, perhaps it would be easier to gain attention, but a simple reader review is way better than what any top publisher can offer...

Readers like yourself are what make the biggest difference to an author, and if you've enjoyed this book and wouldn't mind spending a few minutes leaving a review, it would help me out immensely.

Also by Shawna Coleing

Underwood Series

Christian Thriller

UNDER THE VEIL (book 1)

UNDER FIRE (book 2)

UNDER SIEGE (book 3)

Shadow Alliance Series

Christian Romantic suspense

SHADOW GAME (book 1)

SHADOW LINE (book 2)

SHADOW BREAK (book 3)

SHADOW TRACE (book 4)

Hidden Alliance Series

Christian Romantic Suspense

HIDDEN TRIAL (book 1)

HIDDEN DEPTHS (book 2)

HIDDEN ASCENT (book 3)

HIDDEN CHANCE (book 4)

Bristol Kelley Duology

A clean romantic suspense
SLEIGHT OF HAND (book 1)
SMOKE AND MIRRORS (book 2)

Erin Hart Duology

A clean romantic suspense
OUT ON A LIMB (book 1)
CUT TO THE CHASE (book 2)

About the Author

Shawna Coleing is the author of the Shadow Alliance Series. You can find her on her website or feel free to contact her by email at:
shawnacoleing@pgturners.com

Otherwise you can connect with her here:

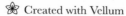 Created with Vellum

Made in the USA
Coppell, TX
21 June 2023

18357555R00184